A Country Idyl

And Other Stories

Sarah Knowles Bolton

A Country Idyl and Other Stories

Copyright © 2020 Bibliotech Press
All rights reserved

ISBN: 978-1-64799-242-2

CONTENTS

A COUNTRY IDYL

IN THE midst of New England mountains, covered with pine and cedar, lies the quiet town of Nineveh, looking towards the sea. Years ago it had mills where lumber was sawed and grain was ground; but now the old wheels alone are left, the dams are broken, and the water falls over the scattered rocks, making music in harmony with the winds among the pines. The houses have gone to decay; the roofs have fallen in, leaving the great, rough chimneys standing like the Druid towers of Ireland.

In one of these old houses, before the young men of New England had gone West to seek their fortunes, lived a miller and his wife. The Crandall family were happy, save that no children had come into the home. Finally a sister of the wife died, bequeathing her little girl to the Nineveh household.

Nellie Crandall grew from babyhood the picture of health, an innocent, cheerful girl, in sweet accord with the daisies of the fields and the old-fashioned flowers she cared for in her foster-mother's garden.

In the house across the way lived John Harding, a tall, awkward boy, the pride of the country school for his good scholarship, and in principle as strong as the New England hills he lived among.

John and Nellie had played together from childhood. He had made chains for her neck of the pine needles; she had fastened golden coreopsis in his homespun coat; and, while no word had been spoken, the neighboring people expected that a new house would sometime be built in Nineveh, and a young couple begin anew the beautiful commonplaces of life.

There was considerable excitement one morning in the quiet town. Byron Marshall, a city youth, had come to Nineveh to visit the Monroe family, cousins of the Hardings. Byron was a handsome, slender lad, well-mannered, just leaving college and ready for a profession. He met Nellie Crandall, and was pleased with the natural country girl.

"No good'll come of it," said one of the old ladies of Nineveh. "I never believed in mismating. John Harding would give his life for that girl, while the city youth, I know, is a selfish fellow."

The summer wore away with rides and picnics, and if John's heart was pained at the attentions given to Nellie, and accepted by her, he said nothing.

1

After Byron's return to the city a correspondence was begun by him.

One Sunday evening, when John came as usual to see Nellie, and they were sitting in the moonlight beside the old mill at the bridge, he said abruptly, "I'm going away from home, Nellie. I have begun to think you wouldn't mind since Byron came."

"But I do mind," said the girl. "I like Bryon, and he seems fond of me; but, John, I don't want you to go, we've been such good friends."

"Yes, but we must be all in all to each other or I can't stay. I've loved you all these years with never a thought of another. I've loved every flower in your garden because you have tended it. This old mill seems precious because you have sat here. All Nineveh is sacred to me because it is your home, but I cannot stay here now."

Nellie was young; she had seen little of the world, did not know the true from the false, and, half captivated with the college youth, she dare not give her promise to John.

They parted in the moonlight, he heavy of heart at going and she regretting that two loved her. John went to a distant State and found employment. No word came from him, and Nellie, who missed him sadly, depended more than ever on the letters which came from Byron.

The next summer Byron spent at Nineveh, and it was talked about the little town that Nellie was engaged, and would soon be a city lady, living in comfort and prominence.

Two years later there was a wedding at the Crandall home, and the pretty bride said good-by to the old mill and the great pines, and left the miller and his wife desolate. Two years afterwards, when she brought back a little son, named Samuel, after the miller, they were in a measure comforted, though they never liked Byron as well as John, "who was of their kind."

When John Harding knew that Nellie was really lost to him and married to another, he, longing for companionship, married a worthy girl, prospered in business, and was as happy as a man can be who does not possess the power to forget. He had learned what most of us learn sooner or later—that life does not pass according to our plan, plan we ever so wisely; that, broken and marred, we have to take up the years and make the mosaic as perfect as we can.

As time passed some of the Nineveh families died, and some moved away to other and busier scenes. Samuel Crandall had been laid in the little cemetery, and Mrs. Crandall was more lonely than ever.

One night there came a wagon to the door, and Nellie

Marshall, her face stained with tears, alighted, with her three children. "We have come to stay, mother," said the broken-hearted woman. "Byron has gone, nobody knows where. He has used the money of others, and we are penniless."

Mrs. Crandall wept on her daughter's neck, as she told somewhat of the hardships of her life with her unfaithful and dishonest husband.

Other years passed, and another grave was made beside that of Samuel Crandall, and Mrs. Marshall, now grown white-haired, lived for her three children, and reared them as best she could in their poverty.

One day there was a rumor in the town that John Harding was coming to Nineveh on a visit. He was well-to-do now, and would come in a style befitting his position. Mrs. Marshall wondered if he would call upon her, and if he would bring Mrs. Harding to see the woman so changed from her girlhood in looks, but nobler and sweeter in character.

Mr. Harding had been in Nineveh for a week. Nellie Marshall had heard of it, and her heart beat more quickly at any footstep on the threshold. One moonlight night she could not resist putting just one spray of golden coreopsis in the buttonhole of her black dress, for if he should come that night he would like to see it, perhaps; for, after all, women do not forget any more than men.

About eight o'clock there was a knock at the door; she was agitated. "Why should I be? He is married," she assured herself.

She opened the door, and John, grown stouter in form and more attractive in face than ever, stood before her. He met her cordially, talked with the children, and seemed more joyous than when a boy.

"And where is Mrs. Harding?" Nellie finally found the courage to ask.

"She is not with me," was the answer.

The call, really a long one, seemed short.

"When do you leave for the West, Mr. Harding?" She had almost said "John," for she had thought of him all these years by the old familiar name.

"Not for two or three weeks, and I shall see you again."

Day after day passed, and he did not come. And now she realized, as she had never before, that this was the only man she had ever loved; that his presence made day, his absence night; that she had loved him from childhood. And now all was too late.

The time came for him to return to the West, and once more he stood by the flower-beds along the walk to the Nineveh house,

3

this time just as the sun was setting over the cedars. He kissed the children. "I have none of my own," he said, and took Nellie's hand, holding it a little longer than he had held it before. Her lips trembled, and her eyes must have told all her heart.

"I have felt so deeply for you," he said; and his own voice grew tremulous. "And will you let me leave this little remembrance for the children?" He slipped a roll of bills into her hand, and was gone in a moment.

Weeks passed, and finally a letter came. She knew the handwriting. What could John wish of her? Perhaps he was inclined to adopt one of her children, and, if so, which could she spare?

Not the oldest boy, for he was her pride; not the second, a girl, who was her comfort and companion; not the youngest, for somehow he looked like John, and he was dearer to her than all beside. When Byron was unkind her heart always turned to John, and perchance stamped her thoughts upon the open, frank face of her youngest child.

She put the letter in her pocket; she must be calm before she read it. She would go out and sit by the mill where he and she sat together. She opened it there and read:

> *My dear old-time Friend: I am alone in the world. I told you my wife was not with me. She died some years ago. I wanted to see if you loved me, as I believed you did. I hope and believe you do still. You know me better than any one else, and you know whether I should care tenderly for your children. If you are willing to come and brighten my home, say so. How I longed to fold you in my arms as I left you, but restrained myself! Telegraph me if I shall come to take you.*

A message was sent from Nineveh: "Come."

The Crandall home has fallen like the others. The flower-beds have vanished, save here and there a self-sown golden coreopsis grows among the weeds. The moon shines silently upon the mill as of old. The few remaining aged people of Nineveh still tell of the faithful love of John Harding for the miller's adopted daughter.

THE SECOND TIME

THE HON. John Crawford had become a prominent man in his community. He had begun life in poverty, had learned economy early, and fortunately had married a girl with tastes and habits similar to his own. Both desired to rise in the world, and she, forgetting herself, bent all her energies toward his progress and success. She did her own housework for years, made her own clothes and those of her children, and in every way saved, that John might be rich and influential. Her history was like that of thousands of other New England women—she wore herself out for her family. She never had time for social life, and not a very great amount of time for reading, though she kept up as well as possible with the thought of the day; but her one aim was to have her husband honored.

John Crawford was a good husband, though not always considerate. He thought nobody quite so good and helpful as Betsey, nobody cooked so well, nobody was more saving, and he was proud to rise by her help. He failed sometimes to consider how large a matter that help had been in his life. If he had been asked who made his money he would have replied without hesitation, "I made it." That Betsey was entitled to half, or even a third, would never have occurred to him. He provided for her and the children all they seemed to need. He was the head of the family, and that headship had made him somewhat selfish and domineering.

As the children grew older, and Mrs. Crawford looked out into the future and realized the possibility of leaving the world before her husband, she thought much of their condition under a changed home. Mr. Crawford would marry again, probably, and her children might have little or none of the property which they together had struggled to earn.

One evening she said, as they sat before the open fire, the children having gone to bed: "John, it seems to me things are unequal in the world. You and I have worked hard, and I have been proud to have you succeed. We both love the children, and want everything done for them. What if I should die, and you should marry again and have other children?"

"Why, Betsey! You don't think I could forget our own precious children? No second wife could or would influence me against my children. You and I have worked together, and I should feel

5

dishonorable to leave them helpless and care for others. You must think me a villain."

"Oh, no, John! But I have seen cases like that. Only the other day the Rev. Cornelius Jones married a young wife, and gave her all his property, leaving nothing to his three daughters. Now, if a minister would do that, what should we expect of others?"

"There must have been peculiar circumstances. He could not have been in his right mind."

"You know, John, if you were to die I should receive a third of what I have helped you earn, and the rest would go to the children; while if I were to die nothing would go to the children. I should like to have at least the third which the law considers mine go to them at my death, as it does in some countries of the Old World, where a man cannot marry a second time till he has settled a portion on his first children."

"But that would be a great inconvenience," replied Mr. Crawford. "A man has money in business, and to take out a third if his wife dies might sadly embarrass him. Or even the use of a third, set apart for them, might cripple him."

"Better that there be a little inconvenience than a wrong done to children," said Mrs. Crawford. "The husband may lose every cent of what the wife has struggled and saved all her life to help him accumulate. Marriage is a partnership, and, like other partnerships, must suffer some change and inconvenience, it may be, if one of the partners dies. There must, necessarily, be a new adjustment of interests."

"But the law allows you to make a will and give away your property, my dear, just as it does me."

"Yes, what I have inherited before or since my marriage; but I have inherited none, and you have not. We have made ours together, and you have often said that you owe as much to my skill and economy as to your foresight and ability."

"And so I do, it is true; but the law makes no provision about our common property."

"But make it yourself then, John, if the law does not. Make a will so that in case of my death my two daughters shall have at least a third of all you are worth at that time, or, if you prefer, put a third—I might feel that it ought to be half—in my name, or perhaps the home, and let that go to our daughters."

"But if I put the home in your name, so that in case of losses something would be saved from creditors, I should want it willed back to me at your death, so that I could still have a home and do as I liked with it."

6

"And then nothing would go to the children at my death? That is not fair, John, and I have worked too hard and long to be willing."

"Well, Betsey, you can trust me to do the right thing. I will think it over," and he kissed her as they closed the not altogether satisfactory conversation.

As was to be expected, Betsey Crawford broke down from the wear and tear of life, and died, leaving her two daughters to the care of a fond and not ungenerous father. The loss was a great one to John Crawford. She had been his competent adviser, with tact and good sense to keep matters right. She had guided more than he ever suspected. He mourned her sincerely, as did her two devoted daughters.

He was lonely, and in time married again, a woman considerably younger than himself, a member of the same church, an ambitious and not over-scrupulous woman. When her son was born she became desirous that every advantage should be placed before him, that he might attain to wealth and honor. She convinced Mr. Crawford in a thousand nameless ways that the boy would need most of the property for business, to marry well, and to carry down the family name. The girls would doubtless marry and be well provided for by their husbands. She talked with Mr. Crawford about the uncertainty of life, and, with tact, urged that other things besides a spiritual preparation for death were necessary. A man should think of the younger members of his family who would be left comparatively helpless.

People said that the strong-willed John Crawford had become very much under the sway of his younger wife; that he had grown less dominant, more appreciative, and more thoughtful of her needs and wishes. He idolized his son, but he seemed no dearer than the daughters of Betsey. He was a more expensive child, for he needed all sorts of playthings, the best schooling, the best clothes, and a somewhat large amount of spending money. It was evident that John Crawford, Jr., would require more money than his half-sisters.

In course of time, Mr. Crawford, having served a term in Congress through good ability and the discreet use of money in organizing his forces, and having done well for his constituency, followed Betsey to the other world. To the surprise of all save the second Mrs. Crawford the property was left to her and her son, with the merest remembrance to the unmarried daughters of hard-working Betsey Crawford.

"I wouldn't have thought it," said a prominent lady in the church. "Why, John Crawford was a deacon, and professed to live according to right and justice! There must have been undue influence. His first wife worked like a slave to help earn that money. I never supposed a man would be unfair to his children."

"You never can tell what folks will do," said another church member. "Youth and tact are great forces in the world. John Crawford never meant to be unjust, but he couldn't help it. A third of that property ought to have gone to those daughters. Why didn't his wife make him fix it before she died?"

"Maybe she tried, who knows?" said the person addressed. "If the law didn't make him do his duty, how could you expect his conscience to do it? We need some new laws about the property which men and women earn together."

Mr. Crawford's injustice resulted in the early death of one daughter, and left bitter memories of her father in the heart of the other.

FIFTEEN THOUSAND DOLLARS

JASON and Eunice Kimball had always longed for money. They had spent their fifteen years of married life on a New England farm, with all its cares and hardships, its early rising, long hours of labor, and little compensation.

The white house, with its green blinds, roof sloping to the rear, and great fir-trees in the front yard, had grown dingy with dust and rain, and there had been no money to repair it.

The children, Susie, James, and little Jason, fourteen, twelve, and ten years old, had worked like their thrifty parents, gaining the somewhat meagre schooling of a half-deserted New England town.

Now a great change had come to the Kimball family. A relative had died and had left to Mrs. Kimball fifteen thousand dollars. It seemed an enormous amount in one way, but not enormous in another. The children must be better dressed and prepared for college, the father must give up the slow gains of the farm and go into business, and Mrs. Kimball must make herself ready in garb and manner for the new life. It was evident that they must move to some village where schools were good and business would be prosperous. What town and what business? These were the exciting topics that were discussed by night and by day. Jason knew how to till the soil, to harvest grain, to be an industrious and good citizen and a kind husband, but he knew little about the great world of trade.

"I might buy out a small grocery, Eunice," said the husband one evening. "People must eat, whether they have decent clothes or books or schools."

"Ah, if you once looked at Mr. Jones's books and saw the uncollectible bills, even from so-called 'good families,' you would not undertake that business!"

"I might buy a tract of land in a growing town and sell lots."

"But what if a panic came, and you lost all?" said the conservative wife.

As soon as it became known that the Kimballs had fallen heir to fifteen thousand dollars, Mr. Kimball was besought on all sides to enter one kind of business or another. One applicant had invented a unique coffee-pot, which would make good coffee out of even a poor berry, and a fortune could certainly be made, if only capital were provided. Another person had a new style of wash-boiler, and experimented with it on Mrs. Kimball's kitchen stove, breaking

9

every lid in the operation. Fortunes seemed lying about at every corner of the street, and the only wonder was that everybody did not get rich. Mr. Kimball was besought to take out life insurance, to buy acres of land in the far West, unseen by buyer or seller, to give to every charity within the State, where-ever the knowledge of the fifteen-thousand-dollar inheritance had permeated.

Finally the town for a home was decided upon, and the business—that of selling coal.

A pretty house was purchased, his children placed in school, a seat in church rented, and a shop for the sale of hard and soft coal.

Mr. Kimball knew nothing of the coal business; but he formed a partnership with a man who knew everything about it—in fact, too much, for at the end of a year the firm failed, the five thousand dollars that Mrs. Kimball gave to her husband having melted away like snow in spring.

Mrs. Kimball's patience had not increased with her gift of money. She blamed her husband for losing, blamed herself for giving the money to him, blamed the world in general.

Mr. Kimball tried other matters, and failed. It was difficult to find a situation in which to work for others, as he was of middle age and young men were preferred. He tried life insurance, and either lacked the courage to visit people in season and out of season, or he lacked volume of speech or multiplicity of argument.

It became evident to the neighbors and to the minister of the parish that matters were going wrong in the Kimball home. The husband wished to go into business again; the wife felt sure that he would lose, and nothing would be left for the children. They reasoned, they quarrelled, and Mrs. Kimball became ill from anxiety.

At last it was noised about that a separation might come in the divided family. Friends interposed, but nothing satisfactory was accomplished. The few thousands that remained were safe in the bank; and this amount Mrs. Kimball had decided should not be touched.

One morning the little village was thrown into consternation. The bank had lost all its funds through the speculation of one of its officers. Save for the little home, the Kimballs were penniless.

Sorrow is sometimes a great strengthener. Mrs. Kimball rose from her illness to face the problems of life. Both parents loved their children, and they were too young to be thrown upon the world.

"Let us sell our home," said Mrs. Kimball, "buy back the old farm, and live together till the end."

And Jason said, "Yes, wife, we shall be happier in the old place without the fifteen thousand dollars."

THE RING OF GOLD

MARTIN DALY had become discouraged. Like many another miner in the far West, he had made money and lost it, had prospected for mines, found ore, and been cheated out of his rights, had grown poor and ill, and had thrown himself under a tree, careless whether he lived or died.

The great snowy mountain-peaks and the rich verdure had lost their attraction for him. He had hoped and been disappointed so many times that he had come to believe himself unlucky; that he should never possess a dollar; that there was neither happiness nor home for him.

He had seen more prosperous days. His large dark eyes, his broad brow, his well-shaped mouth and chin, bespoke refinement in the years that were gone. He had been well educated, had tried many things and failed in them, not from lack of energy nor from lack of judgment, but his fate seemed to be an adverse one.

He had done many good acts, had always helped his brother miners, had tried to look on the bright side of life, had fought manfully, and been defeated in the battle. He had imagined sometimes that the clouds had a silver lining, but the storms always came sooner or later. He meditated thus as he lay under the tree, and finally, more dead than alive from want and exhaustion, fell asleep.

Two men passed along under the brow of the mountain, by the tree. They were tall and straight, and from their dark hair and skin it was easy to perceive their Indian blood.

"The white man is dead," said one of the men, as he bent on his knee beside the sleeper.

"No, there is a twitching of the eyelids," said the other. "He is pale and sick. I will take him home, and Mimosa will care for him."

The conversation, carried on in a low tone, awakened the miner.

"Come with us, and you shall have food and shelter," said the friendly Indian.

Scarcely able to bear his weight, Martin leaned upon the arms of the two men, and soon found himself in the humble Indian cabin.

"Mimosa, here is a stranger. Take care of him. Red Cloud never left a human being to die. He will get well, and then we will send him back to his people."

11

A shy, pale Indian girl came forward and did as she was bidden. She did not speak, but looked very pityingly out of her fawn-like dark eyes. When Martin had been placed in the simple bed she prepared food for him, and fed him as though he were a child. Day by day she came and went, speaking little, but doing gently the things which only a woman's hands can do.

After a time the miner, still a young man, gained in strength, and began once more to hope for a successful future.

"Mimosa," he said one day, "I owe my life to you, and if I am ever rich I will come back and reward you."

"I shall miss you," said the girl shyly. "But I want no money. I shall be happy because you are well again and happy."

"I shall yet find gold, Mimosa. I used to think I should be rich, and then I became poor and sick and lost heart. You wear a ring on your finger and sometimes a chain about your neck, both of beaten gold. Did the metal come from mines near here?"

"My father gave them to me," she replied, and nothing more could be learned from her on the subject.

"Would you care, Mimosa, if I wore the ring until I went away? Perhaps I can find the place where the gold came from."

"You may wear it till you come back rich," she said, smiling.

Days grew into weeks, and the time drew near for the miner to say good-by to the girl who had become his comrade as well as deliverer. Tears filled her eyes as they parted. "You will forget Mimosa," she said.

"No, I will bring back the ring, and you shall give it to the man who makes you his bride. I shall never forget Red Cloud nor his daughter."

Strong and hopeful again, Martin took up life, obtained work, and believed once more that he should find gold.

But he missed the Indian girl. The pines on the snowy mountain-peaks whispered of her. The evenings seemed longer than formerly; the conversation of the miners less interesting. He was lonely. He was earning a fair living, but of what use was money to him if he was to feel desolate in heart? Mimosa was not of his race, but she had a lovable nature. He remembered that she looked sad at his going away. He wondered if she ever thought about him. If she had some Indian suitor, would she not wish for the ring again? He would like at least to see the man and his daughter who had saved his life. He would carry back the ring. Ah! if he knew where the gold in it came from, perhaps he would indeed become rich, and then who could make him so happy as Mimosa?

12

Months only increased the loneliness in Martin's heart. He was becoming discouraged again. He even began to fear that Mimosa was married, and his soul awakened to a sense of loss. He would go back just once and see her, and on his journey back he would sit for a half-hour under the tree where Red Cloud had found him.

"What ails Martin?" said one miner to another. "He must be in love—no fun in him as in the old days. Going to quit camp, he says."

After Martin had decided to go to see Red Cloud his heart seemed lighter. If Mimosa were married he could at least show her his gratitude. And if she were not? Well, it would be very restful to see her once more!

He started on his journey. The full moon was rising as he neared the old tree where Red Cloud had found him. As he approached he was startled by a white figure. He turned aside for a moment, and then went cautiously up to the great trunk. Two dark eyes full of tears gazed up into his eyes, at first with a startled look and then with a gleam of joy and trust.

"Mimosa!" he exclaimed, and clasped the Indian girl in his arms. "Why are you here, child, at this time of night?"

"I came here to think of you, Martin, and the moonlight is so sweet and comforting. The green trees and the mountains tell me of you."

"I have brought you back the ring, Mimosa."

"And are you rich yet? You were to keep it till you were rich."

"No, but I would be rich, perhaps, if you would tell me where the gold in the ring was found."

"My father gave it to me," she replied quietly.

"Mimosa, would you love me if I were rich?"

"Perhaps I should be afraid of you if you were."

"Would you love me if I remained poor as I am now?"

"Yes, always."

"And if I became sick and could not care for you, what then?"

"I would care for you, Martin."

"I have brought back the ring, Mimosa, that you may give it to the man who shall make you his bride."

"And would you like to keep the ring yourself, Martin?"

"Yes, dearest."

They went back to the home of Red Cloud, happy because promised to each other in marriage.

After a quiet wedding Mimosa said one day: "Come with me,

13

Martin, and I will show you where the gold in the ring and the necklace were found."

Not very far from the tree where the miner had lain down discouraged Mimosa pointed out the shining ore, the spot known only to the few Indians.

"Mimosa, there is a mine here! This gold is the outcropping of the veins. I shall yet be rich, my darling."

"Would you surely love me as much, Martin, if you were rich?"

"I would give you everything your heart desired."

"And not go to an Eastern country, and be great, and forget Mimosa?"

"Never!"

With a happy heart Martin Daly took his pick to the mountains. The golden ore opened under his touch. His claim each day showed more value. He had, indeed, become rich through the ring of Mimosa.

Times have changed. The children of the Indian girl, educated, gentle as their mother and energetic as their father, are in a handsome house. Love in the home has kept as bright as the gold in the mountain.

FOUR LETTERS

DEAR ERNEST: I am sitting under a great oak this summer afternoon, just as the sun is setting. The western sky is crossed with bands of brilliant red and yellow, while overhead, and to the east, pink fleecy clouds are floating like phantom ships of coral. The green forest of beech and oak at my right mellows in the deepening gray of the twilight, and the white mansion at my left, with its red roof, looks like some castle in a story. The grand blue lake in the distance seems closer to me in the subdued light, and I almost question if this be a picture or reality.

How I wish you were here to sit beside me, and talk as we used to do in college days! Then we wondered where each would be, what experiences would fill each heart, and what the future had for us in its shadowy keeping.

You have been a wanderer, and seen much of the world. I have had, for the most part, a quiet life of study, have finished a book, have had anxieties, as who has not, but, best of all, I have found my ideal.

You will perhaps smile at this, and recall to me my love of athletic sports, my disregard of the affections, my entire ability to live without the gentler sex. Not that you and I both did not admire a brilliant eye, or a rosy lip, or a perfect hand, but life was so full without all this that we looked at women as one does at rare pictures—expensive luxuries, to be admired rather than possessed.

But all has changed with me. I have met one who will, I think, fill my vision for life. She is not strictly beautiful. Her blue eyes are calm and clear. Her manner is not responsive, and she would seem to a stranger like one to be worshipped from afar. She has depth of affection, but it is not on the surface.

Edith Graham is to most persons a mystery. She loves nature, sits with me often to enjoy these wonderful sunsets, makes me feel that I am in the presence of a goddess, and goes her way, while I continue to worship her.

Yes, I think I have used the right word—"worship." I walk a thousand times past the house where she lives because she is there. I linger in the pathways where she daily walks, with the feeling that her footsteps have given them a special sacredness. I know well the seat in the forest near here where she comes to read and look upon the distant lake. Every friend of hers is nearer to me because her

15

friend. The graves, even, of her dear ones are precious to me. Every tree or flower she has admired is fairer to me. The golden-rod of the fields I keep ever in my study because she loves and gathers it. I have planted red carnations in my garden because she delights to wear them. The autumn leaves are exquisite to me because she paints them, and I recall the sound of her feet among the rustling leaves with the same joy which I feel in remembering the music of the priests of Notre Dame, or the voices of the nuns of the Sacré Cœur in Rome, at sunset.

The moon, from new to full, has an added beauty because when Edith and I are separated she speaks to us both the eternal language of love. When I watch the clouds break over her majestic face I know that Edith too enjoys the beauty of the scene.

The song of the robins among our trees is sweeter because Edith hears it. The little stream that wanders near us and glides over the stones at the foot of the hill in a white sheet of spray is a bond between us, for we have both looked upon it. Edith's name seems as musical to me as the waterfall. I can fancy that it is graven upon my heart.

I know every change of her features,—she is almost always quiet,—and her every word and act I have gone over and over in my mind ten thousand times. We have read together, and I hope she loves me. This companionship is so blessed that I dread to speak to her of love—though my face must always tell it—lest, possibly, the dream be dispelled, and I wake to the dreadful knowledge that she cannot be mine.

Do you know all these feelings, Ernest? Whatever you may think of me, I have grown a nobler man through them. All womanhood is more sacred to me. I can do work I never thought myself capable of before. It would be a pleasure to work for Edith as long as I live. I am going to Europe soon, and I must settle this matter. I will write you then.

Yours,
John.

Dear Ernest: The scene has changed since I wrote you months ago. I am at the foot of the Jungfrau, whose snowy top, gilded by the sun, is ever a thing of beauty.

The day I dreaded has come and gone. I have told Edith all my heart, and, alas! she is not mine. She was already half plighted to a young naval officer, whom she met when she was away at school. I believe she was fond of me, for our tastes are similar, but she has been the true woman through it all.

16

I blame her? Never! I would not allow my heart to cherish such a thought for a moment.

Do I love her less? No. Shall I think a flower less beautiful and fragrant because another owns it and enjoys it? Edith will be to me ever the same lovely picture of youthful womanhood—the same blessing, though to me unattainable. Do not imagine that I shall forget her. A man loves as deeply as a woman, often more deeply, and not seldom remembers as long as she does. Other faces may interest me; other women be companionable; but they will not be Edith.

I shall go back to our old home beside the lake, because she will sometime come there, and it will always be a comfort and pleasure to see her, even if she does not see me. Perhaps it is a foolish wish, but I shall hope sometime to rest in the same cemetery where she rests.

I love to think of her the last thing as I sleep, for then ofttimes in my dreams she talks and walks with me, and I awake refreshed by the memory.

Some one has said, "Happiness is not possession. It is giving and growing;" and I know that I am growing more fit for her companionship, even though it come only in another life.

The seas she sails upon, the harbors she enters, will all be nearer and dearer to me. The world will grow larger instead of smaller to my vision. I shall be lonely; yes, almost unbearably lonely. But, after all, what a blessing to have known her—to have loved her—to have offered her the best thing a man can offer a woman, the consecration of his life to her! What if I had gone through these years and not have seen such an ideal? How poor would be my heart! Now I can say with Shelley, "Love's very pain is sweet."

Of course I can but think of what I have missed. To have seen her in a pleasant home and to come to her after the day's work was done would have been bliss indeed. To have seen the sun set and the moon rise; to have walked over the hills and meadows together; to have read by our open fire; to have laughed and wept and prayed and grown gray-haired together—all this would have made life complete. Even silence together would have made earth seem heaven.

Life is indeed a mystery. It brings us development, if not happiness. For a time after I left home I seemed unable to put myself to any labor, but I have come to be grateful that for me there is so beautiful an ideal—one that sheds a halo about even the saddest day. But there come times of anguish, when I long to hold Edith's hand in mine; to press her to my heart with all the rapture of a perfect love. Then I go out under the blue sky and walk, if I can, always towards the sunset, getting out of the rich color all the balm possible for an unsatisfied soul.

I sometimes wonder if she realizes how I worship her—if she knows all the bliss of loving, and the eternal sorrow of losing. Ah! I know it all.

Yours always,
John.

Dear Ernest: How the years have come and gone since I wrote you from Switzerland! I have just seen Edith home from a voyage to Japan. And she has brought her little girl of three, with her own blue eyes and the same reserved, quiet ways. The child came across the hill with her nurse to our grove, and I made friends with her and held her on my knee and kissed her. She could not know how very dear she is to me, and why. She could not guess that the golden hair which I fondled took me back to other days, and quickened the flow of blood in my veins. Her smooth, fair skin is like her mother's. I could not help wishing that she might stay with me forever, and look out upon the lake and the sunsets.

It will be a dreadful wrench to my heart when they go back. Japan is so far away. Edith looks paler than formerly, and smiles less frequently. I have heard it hinted that she is not happy. Can it be possible that her husband does not appreciate the treasure which he has won?

If I could only speak a word of comfort to her—but that cannot be. She is very pleasant, but calm, with me, and seems glad to have me love her little daughter. I thought I saw tears in her eyes as we sat with the child between us under the oak last night at sunset, but she rose hastily, and said she should take cold in the falling dew.

She is more beautiful to me than when a girl. Her face has more of thought and feeling in it, and a trace of suffering as well, and that heightens her beauty to me, and to men generally, I think. We love to care for others, especially if they need our care, if there is any manhood in us.

Ah, there is nothing on earth so interesting as a woman, with her tenderness, her solicitude for our welfare, her quiet reserve, her gentle listening, her brightness, her nobleness, her grace!

After Edith left me, taking her little girl by the hand, I confess I was desolate, overwhelmingly desolate. Why is it that one person can make night seem day to us; can bring perfect rest and content? I should not have cared if years could have passed while we sat there together. She will go away soon, and I shall have to fight the old battle with self over again, and conquer, and go back to daily duties.

Come and see me here at this lovely outlook. I will show you her child's picture—so like the mother. What will the end be? I suppose you ask. The same as now, probably. I do not look for anything different. I try to be happy and thankful that I live in the same world and now and then in the same city with Edith.

Faithfully,
John.

Dear Ernest: You and I are growing older, but we have kept the same true friendship through all the years. Your life has been full of love and sunshine, and mine so desolate, except for one ennobling affection.

But a great change has come into my life. Edith has come back with her daughter, and both are in mourning. They have been here for months, but I have seen little of them.

A few evenings ago I sat with them among the trees surrounding their lovely home, and as I left I dared to tell Edith that I had not buried all hope for the future. She looked at me gravely, I thought with an appealing expression in her blue eyes, as though she longed for a place where her heart might rest. You know how the eyes can speak volumes. I had never seen her look thus before. Every woman loves to be worshipped. "She must at least be gratified that I love her," I said to myself.

****

I have been to see Edith this evening at sunset. She and I have walked in the ravines, and I have pushed away the underbrush from her lovely head, and told her that I longed to care for her always, and she has laid her white hand on my arm and said, "I love you."

I scarcely know what I am writing. To have her and her child in my home forever! To have the peace and satisfaction and rest of a reciprocal affection! To have her mine to kiss and be proud of, and to live for! To gather golden-rod and carnations for her as when she was a girl! To see the curling smoke of ships on the blue lake, and the golden sunsets, and the rich autumn coloring together, and to know that we shall live side by side till death parts us, and then shall rest together under the same myrtles and red berries of the mountain ash in the cemetery!

Life has begun anew. I seem almost a boy again, while Edith is sweet and grave and happy. I sometimes half fear that it is a dream, it is all so beautiful. The world never seemed half so attractive as now. Come and see us in our home.

Ever yours,
John.

REWARDED

THE SNOW was falling on Christmas eve in the little village of West Beverly. A good many young people were disappointed as they watched the feathery crystals come floating down from a sky that seemed full of snowbanks. They wished to go to a party, or concert, or home gathering, and who could tell whether Christmas would be stormy and disagreeable?

Widow Wadsworth sat in her plain home with her four children, whose faces were pressed against the window pane, guessing what the coming day would bring. Not presents, no; the Wadsworths were too poor for those. But if the day were sunny the sleigh bells would ring, and the poor could slide and make merry as well as the rich.

Hugh, a bright boy of sixteen, had finished his education. By hard work his mother had helped him through the High School, and now he was ready to do his part in the world's work. Not that he did not long for college. Other boys had gone out from West Beverly across the hills to Amherst and to Harvard, but they had fathers to assist them, or kind friends who had furnished the money. Hugh must now aid in the support of his two sisters and little brother.

He had earned something by working Saturdays, so that when Christmas morning dawned Kate Wadsworth found some plaid for a new dress outside her door, Jenny a doll, and Willie a sled.

Mrs. Wadsworth's eyes filled with tears as she kissed Hugh. "It will all come right in the end," she said. "I wish you could go to college, but many a man succeeds without it, and educates himself. It is blessed that we are alive and well, and are able to work. There is as much room in the world for my children as for anybody's. You have been a noble son, and we all love you. I wanted to buy you something, but the money had to go for rent."

"Oh, never mind, mother! I don't need anything. I'm going over to Mr. Carter's to see if they want the snow shovelled from their walks. Tell Willie to come over with his new sled and see me work." And Hugh's big blue eyes brightened as he stepped out into the frosty air. Blessed hope of youth, that carries us into the realities of middle life stronger and happier for the burdens that must be borne!

The Carter mansion away on the hills belonged to the Hon. William Carter, owner of the woollen mills. A man of kind heart, good to his employees, he had always felt an interest in Hugh because the father had worked in his mills. This Christmas morning the Carters wished several walks cleared. The hired man could have done it, but Mr. Carter preferred that Hugh should have the work.

The owner of the woollen mills watched the boy from the window as he shovelled. "A very promising lad," he said to his wife, a little lady much younger than himself. "I wonder what he intends to do in the world," and putting his hands in his pockets he walked up and down the floor. "Jerome Wadsworth was a good workman in the mills. I guess the widow has had a hard time of it since he died."

Mr. Carter walked towards the dining-room, where the breakfast dishes were being removed from the table.

"Margaret, when the boy has finished clearing the walks, send him to me."

"Yes, sir," responded the maid.

An hour later, his cheeks aglow from labor, Hugh stood in the doorway.

"Come in, Hugh, and sit down. What are you going to do?"

"I am ready for any honest work, Mr. Carter. I wanted to go to college, but that is out of the question."

"How much would it cost you?"

"From five to six hundred dollars a year, I suppose."

"Would your mother like to have you go?"

"Very much indeed. She has always wanted it, but I think she really needs my wages now to help her."

"But you can help her better after you have an education. You could earn more, and you would be an honor to her."

"Yes, I know of nothing that would make her so happy."

"Well, my son is young yet, and something may happen which will prevent my sending James to college, so I will send you while I can."

Hugh's blue eyes grew moist. He was indeed to have a Christmas present: a four years' course at college.

"I will come over and talk with your mother about it," said Mr. Carter.

Hugh hurried home, and entered the cottage quite out of breath. Calling his mother aside, he whispered, "Mother, I have a secret to tell you. Mr. Carter is going to send me to college, and then I can better help you and the rest. Just think of it—to have it happen on Christmas Day! And I never expected it."

Mrs. Wadsworth could not speak as she folded her boy in her arms and kissed him. What did it matter to her self-sacrificing heart

22

whether she worked early and late, if Hugh could only be educated! True, he would no longer share her humble cottage, and she would miss his help and companionship, but her life was nothing—his was all. If anything in humanity touches divinity, it is motherhood, that loves and sacrifices without hope of reward.

Busy days followed, when the little trunk was packed, prayers offered, the good-bys said, and her boy Hugh went out into the world.

Four years passed—four years with their new friendships, eager plans, broader outlook, and development of character.

Meantime Widow Wadsworth struggled on, Mr. Carter helping the family somewhat, so that the sisters eventually could fit themselves for teaching. When college days were over another time of anxiety came. Should Hugh have a profession or go into business? He loved books, and finally, after much consideration, he decided to enter the law, working his way as best he could by teaching and writing. Steadily he won success, and before thirty was on the road to fame and fortune.

The years had whitened Widow Wadsworth's hair. All her family were now earning, and life had become easier. The years, too, had brought changes in the Carter family. The woollen mills had failed to bring money to their owner, and the large home had passed into other hands. Pretty Isabel Carter, whom it was whispered Hugh had desired to marry, had thrown herself away on a showy youth, who married her with the expectation of securing a fortune. James Carter, the only son, was working his way through college.

As is often the case, a woman was longing and praying for James's success. Jenny Wadsworth was teaching a village school. She and James Carter had been friends. She knew his many good qualities, and whether he ever cared for her or not she determined that his father's failure should not spoil his life if she could help it. Kate could assist the family, and unbeknown to any one Jenny was saving money for James Carter's education. One morning a letter was sent to Hugh, saying: "James Carter is trying to work his way through college, and we must help him. Here is one hundred dollars which I have saved, and I will send more soon. Do not tell anybody living, but use it for him. Mr. Carter helped you, and I know you will be only too glad to help James. I see him rarely, but he is a noble fellow, and I long to have him succeed. In a little while he can be in the office with you. Your loving sister, Jenny."

Hugh smiled as he read the letter, and blessed woman for her sweet self-sacrifice; but a shadow came over his face in a moment. Perhaps he thought of Isabel, and of his own disappointment.

23

A letter was sent to James the next morning with a check from Hugh and a hundred dollars from "a friend." "Come to me," wrote Hugh, "as soon as you are through college, and let me help to repay a little of the debt I shall always owe your father."

When his course was finished James Carter, manly in physique and refined in face, stood in the doorway of a New York office. He was warmly welcomed by Hugh, who had not seen him for years.

"The debt is more than paid to my father," said James. "I have had your example always before me to surmount obstacles and make a man of myself, and now in turn I hope to help you by faithful labor. I have been curious to learn of the 'friend' who has sent me money. I have thought over all my father's acquaintances and cannot decide who it can be."

"Oh, never mind, James; you will learn sometime perhaps, and it is of no consequence if you do not! The act of giving is what broadens hearts, whether the giver ever be known or not. I promised to keep it a secret."

The two young men went to live in quiet bachelor quarters together. Work, earnest and absorbing, filled the days and often the evenings.

"I have asked mother and Jenny to spend a few days with us," said Hugh one evening. "Jenny teaches in a town not far from here, and my good mother has been visiting her, and will stay here a little on her way to West Beverly."

"That will do us good. I have had so little time to see ladies that it will seem quite a home touch to our bachelor life," responded James.

Mrs. Wadsworth and her daughter came, and a week passed happily. Jenny was intelligent and charming—how could she be other than lovely with such a mother? The four walked in the evenings, Jenny seeming naturally to be left in the care of James, while Hugh delighted in showing attention to his mother. When mother and daughter had gone home the quiet room seemed desolate. Hugh missed them, but James was absolutely homesick. New York, great and fascinating, had lost its attraction. With the departure of one face the sun seemed to fade out of the sky.

"You seem sad, James," said Hugh, as they sat together one evening,—he wondered if Jenny's visit did not have something to do with it,—"and perhaps you better take a few days' vacation and go home."

"I am restless and unhappy; I scarcely know why. I think a change would do me good."

24

James started the next day for West Beverly, but easily persuaded himself that a call on Jenny Wadsworth at the place where she was teaching, if only for a few hours, would make the journey pleasanter. As he surmised, he felt lighter-hearted after his visit with her, especially as he obtained from her a promise that she would correspond with him.

Mrs. Carter, who idolized her son, was made very happy by his coming. When he returned to the city, work seemed less irksome, letters grew singularly interesting and comforting, till one day James said:

"Hugh, there's no use in trying to hide from you the fact that I love your sister Jenny, and wish to marry her as soon as I can support her."

"She loved you long ago, James, but I was not allowed to tell you of it. Are you engaged?"

"Yes."

"Well, you've found out who the 'friend' is, then?"

James Carter turned pale.

"You don't mean that Jenny earned money to help take me through college?"

"Yes."

"Then I will pay her back compound interest, the noble girl."

Years have passed. Hugh, now very wealthy, has never married, but finds a happy home with James and Jenny Carter and their little son Hugh. The Hon. William Carter learned that it pays a thousand-fold to help a boy on in the world, and Jenny rejoices that she, too, helped a young man to success.

THE UNOPENED LETTER

THERE was a carriage waiting at the door, and the servant had just announced to Miss Hamilton that a gentleman had called to see her.

"I will be down in a moment," answered a cheery, blue-eyed girl, as she slipped an unopened letter into her pocket. She had recognized the handwriting as the postman handed it to her. The letter was from a young college senior in the quiet New England town, at home for his summer vacation,—Arthur Ellsworth, a manly fellow, whom she had known and admired from childhood. And now Arthur's brother, Elmer Ellsworth, was waiting to take her for a drive. The latter was the handsomer of the two possibly, with his fine form and dark eyes. He, also, was in the last year of college life.

After pleasant greetings the young people started, in the bright September morning, for the proposed ride. Who that has driven through Lexington and Woburn, past Mystic pond, will ever forget the quiet country roads, the historic associations, the variety of wooded hills and pretty valleys? Now the two schoolfriends talked of the present with its joy and the future with its hopes, of the books they had studied and the plans they had made. Now they gathered golden-rod, and listened to the song of the birds in the bracing air. It was a fitting time to say what had long been in Elmer's heart—that sometime, when his profession had been entered upon, she would be the woman whom he wished to make his wife.

It was a hard matter for her to decide. Both brothers had been dear to her, perhaps Arthur especially,—and both were noble and worthy. Arthur had never spoken to her of marriage; and now Elmer had told her his love, and that she could make him happy. Had Arthur spoken first, perhaps her heart would have more warmly responded; but in the beauty of that autumn morning, with the hopeful, earnest young man by her side, she gave her promise to be his wife.

As soon as she reached her home she ran upstairs, hastily threw off her wraps, and remembered the letter from Arthur, in her pocket. Opening it, she read:

"How many times I have wanted to tell you that I loved you! How often have the words died on my lips! But now, before I go back to college, I must ask you if you can return that love, and sometime be mine."

Alas, that she had not opened the letter sooner! She could not tell Arthur that she had preferred him to Elmer; that were disloyalty to the man whom she had promised to wed. She could only say that she was already betrothed to his brother. She married him whom she had promised. Both men became prominent in the history of New England—this little story is true. One went through life unmarried. His letter was opened too late.

THREE COLLEGE STUDENTS

"WHAT'S the work for vacation, boys?"

The speaker was a tall, dark-haired, open-faced young man, who sat with his two companions on the sloping ground of Amherst College, looking away to silent Mount Tom and the fertile meadows of the Connecticut-river valley.

"It's something downright earnest for me," said James Wellman, a broad-shouldered, big-hearted youth from the neighboring county, who in spite of poverty and many obstacles had fought his way by the hardest work. "I'm in debt for board, books unpaid for; but I've seen worse times than these. I'm used to standing alone, so I'm ready for the battle. I shall take an agency—books, or maybe clothes-wringers, to sell."

"That will be fun, I'll warrant," said the first speaker, Grant Reynolds, whose father, a rich manufacturer, had spared no pains to make his son's life a bed of roses, altogether different from what his own had been.

"Not much fun," said James. "You wouldn't like contemptuous looks from women who know less than you, and whose hearts had become hardened because their husbands, once poor, very likely, had become the possessors of houses on aristocratic streets. Why, a woman—I will not call her a lady—whose husband used to be a stable boy, but who has become a rich government official, ordered me out of the house when I was selling chromos. She said 'agents were tramps and a nuisance;' and when I explained that I was working my way through college, she answered, remembering the former occupation of her lord, perhaps, 'Be somebody's coachman, then, and earn an honorable living.' I wanted to add, 'And run away with your pretty daughter;' but I only replied politely, 'Nobody would hire an inexperienced man for two months, which is as long as our vacation lasts.'"

"But these must be rare cases," said Grant. "Most well-to-do ladies are very courteous."

"Yes, when you meet them on an equality in drawing-rooms; but not always when you are a workingman."

"Well, I'll try it for once. It'll be a fine lark anyway, and I shall learn something of human nature."

"That you will," answered Wellman. "I'll take the country round that aristocratic town down the river, and you may take the stylish avenues. You'll find blue blood in plenty—blue because the

28

fathers owned land there a little before the present generation. Of course, you'll find many well-bred people who are proud of their heads rather than of their purses; but even these are often very 'select.' We profess equality, and are probably more democratic than any other country; but a little extra amount of front lawn, or the fact that our great-grandfather was a governor, or that one woman has 'William Morris' chintz in her chambers, of which, perhaps, her neighbor never heard,—these make various degrees of rank. If our ancestor came over in the 'Mayflower,' or was even a sutler in the Revolutionary war, our fame is unalterably fixed."

"I should like to sell books in so high-toned a town," said Grant. "Maybe I might fall in love with some dainty daughter of a lineal descendant of a governor, or of a stable-boy!"

"Precious little good it would do a book-agent, for you would be classed among poor people if you worked, no matter how rich your father might be."

The conversation had been listened to by a light-haired, blue-eyed student, a poet in temperament and by heredity. He was the only child of a devoted minister of the Gospel, now dead, and of a refined and intellectual mother. She would have shielded him from every rough wind had it been possible, but at best she could only pray for him, and send him now and then a little box of comforts, with her fond and beautiful letters. He worked late at night over his books, and his delicately curved mouth had come to bear an expression of sadness as he looked out upon the struggle before him. Heretofore the little money of the household had sufficed; but now he must earn his bread like James Wellman.

"Cheer up!" said the latter, who had noticed the tell-tale face of the minister's son, Kent Raymond. "Blue eyes and polished manners will win kindness. We all have to get a trifle mellowed. We, who know how to earn our support, get a little extra schooling more than the other boys, that's all. Life is good or bad, just as you look out upon it. It's full of sunshine to me, for I won't look at the shadows."

Vacation days came. Kent and Grant took the book-agency, and James the clothes-wringer, among the country folk, who usually have a kindly interest in a boy who means to be somebody in the world.

****

One bright day soon after, satchels in hand, the two college boys started out along one of the broad avenues of the staid old city.

29

"Don't get discouraged!" said Grant to his boyish companion, who shrank from his task. "Remember you're doing missionary work every time you get a book into a house. We'll report three hours from now at the end of the street."

The first house was of gray stone, set back in the grounds; not belonging to one of the old families, who prefer an old mansion, lest they be counted among the nouveaux riche. Great bunches of varied-colored coleus and red geranium mingled with the greensward like a piece of mosaic. Vines were beginning to grow over the stone porch, and the whole bespoke comfort, even luxury. Kent pulled the bell with a sinking at heart, as he wondered who would appear and what she would say. A servant, not cleanly in apparel, opened the door after long waiting. The true position of a family can generally be seen through its domestics.

"Are the ladies of the house in?" asked the college boy.

"What do you want of 'em?"

"I am selling a valuable book about the 'Home.'"

"No, the missus don't want it. She told me as how she niver let a book-agent inside the door, and she'd scold me if I called her. She niver reads nothin' but a novel—niver," volunteered the loquacious, but kind-hearted girl, despite her torn apron and soiled hands.

At the next mansion Kent was told that the "missus" had gone to the seashore; but the knowing look in the servant's face showed that she had been instructed to make this reply to all callers. It sounded aristocratic to be at Narragansett Pier or on the Atlantic coast, even though finances would not permit of this refreshing journey.

At the next house a kind-faced woman, who really belonged to one of the old families, and felt none too proud to open her own door, bade the young man a pleasant "Good-morning," and though she did not wish to purchase the book, which, though tastefully made, was commonplace in subject, she thanked him for seeing it, and hoped he would sell elsewhere. His heart was a trifle lighter after this kindly greeting, though his purse grew no heavier. At the next house, and the next, he met with the same refusals. Finally, near the end of the street, the colored man who opened the door was also striving to earn money for a college course. He had been two years in Harvard University already. Both father and mother were dead, but from love for a girl who taught a colored school he had become ambitious, and determined to work his way through some institution. The subject of the book touched his heart. Katie, his school-teacher, would like it; the suggestions about husbands

30

and wives, and the words about neatness, culture, and tenderness, would do both good.

"How much is it?" said the colored youth.

"Two dollars."

A disappointed look came into the face of the would-be purchaser.

"I receive seventy-five cents commission," said Kent, "and I will let you have the book for one dollar and a half; that will leave twenty-five cents for my dinner."

"I hate to ask you to take less, sir, but I can't pay two dollars, because I haven't so much. But here's the one-fifty;" and he added, as he held the book tenderly, "Katie will so like it!" When a man is really in love he can't help telling somebody, even though it be a book-agent.

Meanwhile Grant Reynolds had been learning his first experience of work in the broad world, which has too little care for and sympathy with toilers. He soon found that selling books from house to house was no "lark," as he had anticipated. His lips curled in disdain as he was several times addressed rudely by servants, or by women whom he knew were far below him in social position. Did so many fashionable people, then, have two methods of action—one for the rich and the other for the poor?

As he was thus musing, he opened a gate and walked up to a beautiful mansion, Elizabethan in style, that one would imagine to have been just transported from England, with its ivies and great beds of roses. He stopped suddenly, for just before him a fair-haired girl, in simple blue, with broad sun-hat wreathed with daisies, was clipping a bunch of deep-red roses. She looked up half inquiringly, as the young man approached and lifted his hat. He was not abashed—he had seen attractive girls too often for that; but her kind look had an unusual effect after the sharp refusals of the morning.

The frank face of Grant could scarcely help showing its appreciation of both girl and flower, as he said, "I am canvassing for a book: 'The Past, Present, and Future of America.'"

Perhaps the girl did not care much for the book, but she liked the looks of the tall, manly youth before her, and in her heart admired a man who had energy and will enough to earn a living for himself. Most young men whom she had met had leaned upon their fathers; and it was seldom difficult to tell what laurels they would win in the jostle which we call life.

"May I see the book?" she asked, holding out one white hand, while the other clasped the roses.

31

"Can I hold the flowers while you look?" said Grant, while a satisfied expression stole about his mouth and large brown eyes.

"It is beautifully illustrated! I like pictures of people greatly. I am always wondering what they have accomplished, or will in the future."

"Ah! then you are ambitious?"

"Yes; mamma thinks too much so for a girl. I have wanted to go to college," said the natural young woman, "but she thinks it is useless compared with my music."

Grant hoped she would go on artlessly talking about herself, but she suddenly changed the line of thought, as she said: "I am glad to see a book about America—I love our country! I have been with mamma to England and the south of Europe, but I saw nothing so dear as our own country and people. I think our men the noblest in the world."

There was no thought of compliment, for she did not even look toward the young man to whom she was apparently talking. At this moment a woman, handsomely attired, stood in the doorway, and with clouded brow bade her come in.

"I was looking at a beautiful book, mamma," said Marion.

"We want no books of an agent," said the stern, proud woman. "If we need books we buy them at Hamerton's" (one of the largest dealers in the East).

"I am in college," said the young man, piqued at the woman's rudeness, and half angered that the lovely girl should be found fault with. "I am earning some money in this way," he added, not wishing to lie about the matter, and yet rather enjoying this study of human nature.

"I am glad to help poor young men,"—she remembered when the shrewd Mr. Colwell, her husband, made his first dollars in common work at railroading,—"but I never buy of agents! Why, we should be bored to death if we did! Besides, I think our country is running to education. Men who should be West on farms are striving to go through college, and then will starve as poor doctors or lawyers in the busy cities. We need men to build our railroads; Mr. Colwell says men are so scarce and labor so dear that he has to import rough foreigners. Education is the bane of common folks. It spoils our girls. Look at those in our high schools!—they're too good to be servants. While their mothers are toiling over the wash-tub these young misses fit themselves to be teachers. They'd better go West and become farmers' wives. They've got to marry common people, for they can't get rich men."

32

Grant thought to himself how these educated poor girls were to be the great moral force of our country in its grand future; but he made no answer as self-sufficient Mrs. Colwell went on:

"If Marion were to teach, why, all this education would be good for her, perhaps; but my daughter will never be obliged to."

"But you didn't see the book, mamma," pleaded the girl, whose cheeks had become as red as the roses which Grant had handed back to her.

"No; and I've no time for it. Your father is waiting to take you to drive. Besides, I was surprised to see you conversing with a stranger."

The young man lifted his hat to Marion as he passed out of the gate, but not till he had said a word of thanks for her kindness to an unknown student. He thought he saw the blue eyes moisten as they looked up to his, showing that she felt her mother's harshness to a youth who appeared to be working his way alone in the world.

Marion Colwell was not given to sentiment, but she wondered a thousand times what would become of the handsome college boy, and she could not help taking a bud from the flowers which he held for her and pressing it between the leaves of a book, with some tender yet painful recollections. Marion seemed unusually quiet during the ride with her father, but no word was spoken about the book-agent; for Mr. and Mrs. Colwell lived so independently of each other that the daughter never thought of confiding her troubles to either.

At the end of the three hours the two college students met to recount their experiences and successes. Grant had not sold a single book, but he drew from his pocket a red rosebud, and showing it to Kent said: "I'm foolish, I do believe; but I've seen a girl to-day who has paid me a thousand times for all the annoyance of being a book-agent. Perhaps I shall never see her again, but I shall keep in memory one lovely face, and I know she has a noble soul. I took this bud, unbeknown to her, from a bunch I held for her while she looked over that book. I'll not part with the book either, since she has looked at its pictures."

Kent did not make fun of him, for he had a warm heart, and enjoyed the picture which Grant drew of the fair young face. The vacation came to its close. Some money had been made by each of the three students, Grant dividing his equally between James and Kent.

Eight years had come and gone. James Wellman was in business, and had become successful. Kent had graduated with honor, but gone home to his widowed mother to die. Grant had studied theology, and for three years had been settled in a Western city, whither he had been drawn by his friend Wellman. A July morning came like that on which he had passed from house to house along the city streets to sell books. The young minister stood in his accustomed place, about to preach from the well-known text, "Cast thy bread upon the waters; for thou shalt find it after many days." A lady, dressed in blue, who was a stranger to the congregation, entered, and was shown to a seat well in front. She looked long and earnestly at the speaker, as though she was aware whom she had come to hear. For a moment, as the minister caught a glimpse of the face, he changed color, but immediately regained his self-possession.

After the service he stepped directly down to the pew, and the parishioners said to one another: "Why, we didn't know that the new school-teacher, Miss Colwell, was a friend of our pastor!"

He said, as he shook her hand, "I am glad once more to thank you for your kindness of years ago." He spoke slowly, as one who has had hopes and conquered them. "Is your mother with you?" involuntarily rose to his lips.

"No; I am alone, and teaching in your city."

"I have been to your Eastern home, but was told that you had gone West; and further than that I could learn nothing."

And then the past years were gone over. Mr. Colwell had failed, not with honor, and had been glad to go West, as his wife had recommended Grant to do years before, and had become lost in the whirl of a great city. Mrs. Colwell allowed it to be reported that Marion was to marry a rich widower. A wealthy family came to occupy the Colwell mansion, and society interested itself in the new and forgot the old. And now Marion, poor and unmarried, had come to the public school as a teacher.

The minister called often at the school, and finally the gossips suspected that the cause of education was not the only motive for his visits. Once when he called he laid down a pressed and faded red bud. "Do you remember those flowers I held so many years ago?" And, blushing, she told him of a similar one which she treasured.

A look of joy and half surprise came into his face. "Did you, then, think of one whom you supposed a poor boy, Marion?"

"And do you think of one who is in reality a poor girl now?"

The wedding was a quiet one, Marion wearing, at Grant's request, a simple blue dress, with red roses in her hand. What were Mrs. Colwell's thoughts as she looked at the book-agent, now her son, no one could know, for poverty had not made her less proud, but it had doubtless made her more considerate and courteous.

"I would sell books again to find you, Marion;" and her pretty blue eyes looked their happiness in response.

THE TWILIGHT HOUR SOCIETY

"HELÉNA, we must send out the invitations this very afternoon for the new literary society. It must be done with great care, too. I wish this to be the most select club of the West."

The speaker was Mrs. Helen Brunswick, who had just returned from Europe. She was a lady of considerable culture and taste, and, what was not an inconvenient addition, of wealth. Her husband, a good business man, had died—perhaps opportunely; for, though Mrs. Brunswick was polite to him, she told her bosom friends that "he was not poetical," and, therefore, not a very congenial spirit. His wife was a teacher when he married her, poor, but of very good family, and his money was undoubtedly the chief attraction.

She had one child, whose name, for the sake of elegance, she always called Heléna rather than Helen, and of whom she was very fond; but her one absorbing plan was to make her home a literary centre. She bought, on her return from Europe, an old-fashioned house,—a new one would have seemed vulgar to her æsthetic taste,—and furnished it as nearly as possible like the houses of some celebrated persons which she had seen abroad. She revelled in old tapestries, and bronzes which looked as though they were made in the bronze age.

Heléna sat down, note-book in hand, to make out a list of those who were to be honored members of the new association.

"Shall we invite Fanny Green, mamma?"

"Oh, no, dear! She is only a local poet, getting a few articles into the newspapers here and there. This society will not be established to help struggling newspaper writers or embryo artists. These will make their way somehow if they have talent, but the elegant ladies of Lakeville will not care to associate with such crude aspirants. We must take those from the very highest walks of life, those who enjoy art especially, and can prepare an essay on sculpture or Egyptian lore. The young artists and novelists are usually poor and hard workers, so they would have no time to look up these subjects, which require great research and the leisure that only a lady of wealth has."

"But, mamma, it would so help the rising artists if their pictures could be brought before the society. They would be purchased, probably, for the elegant homes."

"Oh, no! Most elegant ladies want a picture painted by a famous artist, so that when they speak of the work to a friend the talent will be seen at once."

"Don't they know talent when they see it, whether John Smith or Bougereau painted it?"

"Oh, dear, no, Heléna! You must not ask too much of people. I don't care to read a book unless a well-known name is on the title-page. I consider it a waste of time. As soon as a man has made his mark I am glad to read him."

The rising artists and the rising editors and contributors were not invited to membership in the new organization. Thirty-five names were sent out.

"We must not have more than twenty-five in the circle, Heléna, for large societies are never select. If there are but a few, and those very literary, they will praise each other and feel proud of the pleasure of belonging. There's everything in knowing how to handle women. Let them think it is exclusive and there will be a great longing to join; and when they cannot be admitted, from the smallness of the number, the society will become the leading topic of the city. Each member, too, will be all the more interested if she takes her turn in writing an essay, and this would not be possible in a large society."

"Why, mother, half of those whom you have named couldn't write an essay!"

"Well, my child, they have some friend who can help them. Money always buys help, and usually of a very superior kind."

The invitations were sent out, and in due time the elegant ladies arrived. They admired Mrs. Brunswick's rugs, her choice bits of needlework from abroad, and especially her antique bronzes.

The first tribulation of the society was over the adoption of a name. The "Mutual Club" was suggested, but "club" seemed strong-minded to some of the ladies present, and was abandoned. One suggested the "Society for Intellectual Growth," but this seemed to suggest labor, and it would not be best to suggest very much work to such a charming circle. Mrs. Brunswick herself suggested, after many others had spoken, that the "Twilight Hour" would be poetic and refining, and as the members would usually come late in the afternoon, or in the evening if some celebrity were invited, this name would cover all times and seasons, convey no impression of moral reforms, and frighten no husbands with the fear that their wives would become unsuited to pretty gowns by mental wear.

This name was voted a happy thought, and the plan

proceeded. A committee on membership was suggested, only twenty having responded to the invitation, and five more could be admitted. One lady, the wife of a senator, must be secured at all hazards, and this committee were to wait upon her at once. Another lady had travelled nearly the world over, and had several millions in her own right, and must on no account be omitted. A third was selected for no especial reason except she had held herself above ordinary society, and the select had come to regard this as a sign of aristocracy. Real aristocracy is too quiet to attract much attention, but the unreal is very prevalent.

The desired number was made up, and the "Twilight Hour Society," as was expected, became the talk of Lakeville. A Gentlemen's Night was given occasionally, and those only were invited who were supposed to be poetic. There was a leaning toward the ministerial profession, and a few judges and doctors were permitted to enter the select circle. The time came when it was necessary to invite a celebrity. Mrs. Wentworth was talking the matter over with Mrs. Brunswick.

"I hear," said the former lady, "that the author of the new book which has just appeared in Boston, "The Story of a Life," is to be at Lakeville soon to visit a cousin. The book is selling rapidly. It is a delightful psychological story of a woman's heart, I have heard, and the men are as eager to read it as the women. Mr. Smithnight, the author, has become famous suddenly, and all the young ladies are enthusiastic over him. He is quite young, and very delightful, they say."

"Oh, yes," said Mrs. Brunswick, "anything that comes from Boston is delightful! Society is very deep there. The people are always making a study of hidden things of the mind, while we at the West are so very practical over the bread and butter matters of life. Alas! how far we are drifting from the beautiful and the sublime! We must have Mr. Smithnight at our next reception, and make it as elegant as possible. How lovely those people are who write books!"

The cousin of Mr. Smithnight, who lived on a side street, and never would have been thought worthy to step into the Twilight Hour circle, was visited, and asked if a reception for Mr. Smithnight could possibly be arranged. The young Plato was glad to be shown off before the admiring gaze of the uncultured West, and readily consented to be present.

"Heléna," said Mrs. Brunswick, as they draped the mantel with smilax and lilies of the valley, "I have always hoped that you would marry an author. Perhaps in Mr. Smithnight you will find your ideal."

"I hope he's handsome, mamma, and not too conceited, as so many literary people are."

"I think you misjudge literary people, dear. They must hold themselves aloof from general society, else they would not be considered so great. You know a writer across the water always seems greater to us than our own authors."

The old-fashioned house of the Brunswicks was lighted, not so gorgeously as to seem loud, and fragrant flowers were in profusion. Very elegant people came in their choicest robes to pay allegiance to the new novelist. Had he been a poet, he must needs have waited till he was fifty for America to find out whether he had genius or no; had he been a scientist, he would not have won his fame till death probably; but having given the public a well-written book which sold, America at once pronounced him a genius. Without doubt there were wheels within wheels which procured its publication. Perhaps he was a cousin to some first-class novelist, or had a governor to recommend his work; for how are publishers to know when a thing will be a success? Nearly all the great books, like "Uncle Tom's Cabin" and "Jane Eyre," have been refused for months, and even years.

Mr. Smithnight was present to receive the homage of Lakeville. He had a fine, even commanding, presence: black hair, which lay lightly over his forehead, a stray lock drooping occasionally, which his white hand tossed back; expressive dark eyes; and a bland smile. He was evidently a good student of human nature, for, while he was egotistical,—successful men usually have a good opinion of themselves,—he had the tact to make every lady feel that the intellectual culture of Lakeville was something phenomenal. Mrs. Brunswick thanked him heartily for coming, coming from such a centre of knowledge as Boston, to stimulate the over-practical West. She wanted to enjoy his conversation at another time, when she and dear Heléna could have him all to themselves. As he took his departure he held Heléna's hand somewhat tenderly, and begged the pleasure of frequent visits during his short stay at Lakeville.

"Heléna," said Mrs. Brunswick, after the guests had departed, "I think Mr. Smithnight the most charming celebrity we have ever had. Think how people will speak of it! I know of nothing so delightful as a salon for literary people. How many must envy me the rare pleasure of bringing together these appreciative people and these great people! You know some of our celebrities from other cities have been so dull and stupid, and read such non-understandable essays, that our ladies have not known what to say or do. I think some of the manuscripts must have lain in trunks for years. But Mr. Smithnight is so charming, so fresh and entertaining! I think he likes you, Heléna, for I saw him bestowing very admiring glances upon you."

"I don't know. I didn't trouble myself much about him. I liked him, though, well enough."

"Oh, you must be very polite to him, my dear, for literary chances are so rare at the West! Think where such a man would place you."

Mr. Smithnight's stay at Lakeville grew from days into weeks, and finally into months. He was a frequent visitor at Mrs. Brunswick's, and rumor whispered that he was to wed Heléna. Mrs. Brunswick made him the lion of the city. She bought sundry copies of the "Story of a Life," and placed them where they would receive glowing notices by the press, and be read by the most select of Lakeville society. She sent several copies abroad, telling the recipients that it was written by a special friend of Heléna's.

Mr. Smithnight had found no such encouraging aid in Boston. There a few mutual friends helped each other, but the outside world troubled itself little about the strugglers for fame. At last it was publicly announced that Mr. Smithnight and Heléna were engaged. Some common-sense mothers wondered if he had the ability to earn a living, knowing that literature in general is not a paying business. Some wondered whether he was able to spend so much as he seemed to be doing weekly; but marrying a young lady well-to-do might be an effective way of meeting debts.

Mrs. Brunswick would have preferred that the young couple live with her, but Heléna wished a house of her own, which was accordingly purchased. Mr. Smithnight, with his refined taste, helped in the selection of the furniture and the bridal trousseau, and did not hesitate to buy the best.

One afternoon, when the last articles had been purchased, a wild rumor was heard on the street that Mr. Smithnight had been seen driving out of town with a lady who was not Heléna Brunswick; that many bills had been contracted in Mrs. Brunswick's name and left unpaid; and that money had been obtained at the bank fraudulently by the departing celebrity.

Mrs. Brunswick was overwhelmed with the news. Heléna was exceedingly annoyed, but in no wise heart-broken, because for years she had liked a poor young artist of the city, who was not thought high enough to be invited to the Twilight Hour Society.

The literary association finally disbanded. Mrs. Brunswick sold the old-fashioned home and moved to another city, holding no more receptions for celebrities. Heléna married her poor artist, who rose to eminence in his profession.

SLAVE AMY

IN NORTH CAROLINA over a century ago lived Mr. John Payne, a wealthy planter, descended from an earl's daughter. He and Thomas Jefferson, who afterwards became President of the United States, both loved the same beautiful girl, Mary Coles. She preferred young Payne, and married him, and became the mother of Dolly, the wife of President James Madison, one of the most beloved women ever in the White House.

Dolly was an uncommonly beautiful child, and her fond mother, lest the sun should tan her face, used to sew a sunbonnet on her head every morning, and put long gloves on her arms when she went to school.

Mr. Payne, her father, a Quaker, became convinced that slavery was a sin, and sold his plantation, freed his slaves, and moved to Philadelphia in 1786. This was just after the Revolutionary war, and the money of the country had become depreciated.

John, his oldest son, was travelling in Europe, and came home to help his father start in business. Neither knew much about close economy, or business methods, or the dishonesty of some of their competitors. After a time Mr. Payne failed, and the rich family was reduced to poverty.

The father sank under his misfortune. A wealthy young man by the name of Todd, of excellent habits, had befriended Mr. Payne in his pecuniary troubles. He wished to marry Dolly, but she did not love him well enough.

The father called the young beauty of nineteen to his dying bed and told her his wish that she should accept John Todd. Dolly consented, and thus made her father's last days happy. Mr. Todd proved a devoted husband, but died of yellow fever three years after their marriage, leaving Dolly with two little children, one a baby of three weeks, who died soon after. Two years later she married James Madison.

Mr. Payne and his beautiful wife, Mary Coles, had always been kind to their slaves, so much so that some refused to leave them, and came to Philadelphia to live in their house.

One poor slave, called "Mother Amy," when freed, went out to service. She saved all her money carefully; nobody could guess for what purpose. She was unlettered, but she had the gratitude and devotion characteristic of her race.

For herself she could endure poverty and not mind it. She did not need or care for fine clothes, but she could not bear that the woman who was once her lovely owner should be in reduced circumstances.

When death came for "Mother Amy" after all the hard years of labor, she left five hundred dollars, which she had struggled all the years to save, to Mrs. Payne, her widowed mistress.

One does not have to look in elegant mansions, or among the educated only, for the noble virtues of self-sacrifice. No character is fine or beautiful without it. "Mother Amy" left a name and example worthy to be remembered.

LIKE OUR NEIGHBORS

"WE MUST have a party," said Mrs. Morris to her husband. "I am under obligations to Mrs. Raymond and Mrs. Nichols, and to no end of ladies who have invited me to their homes."

"I don't see how we can afford it, wife, for times are hard. I haven't made a cent, scarcely, in business during the past year."

"Well, it will never do to let people know that we are straitened. That would hurt your business. Besides, the children are coming on; and I must keep in society for their sakes. I don't want to have a party in a niggardly way, either. We must have the house fixed up to look as well as our neighbors', and I must have my last silk dress made over in the present style."

Mr. Morris sighed, for he found life a struggle. If he had spent money for tobacco, clubs, and the like, there might have been some excuse for Mrs. Morris's lack of economy; but he was careful and saving, and, had his wife been of a similar disposition, they would have been in easy circumstances. As it was, people wondered why she dressed so well, and commented upon it; but she thought they admired her good looks and fine appearance. The world, after all, is fairly sensible, and usually knows better than we think whether people can afford fine houses and fine clothes. There is seldom any great amount of deception.

Mrs. Morris carried her points, as usual. Money was borrowed; the dress was made over; the guests were invited; and the Morris party, with its flowers and supper and display, was the talk of the hour, till it was forgotten in the next sensation.

Mrs. Morris had to go to the seashore every year, because her neighbors did. She left her comfortable home; and for six weeks, while Mr. Morris lived as best he could, she had the joy of staying in a small, inconvenient, unattractive room at a hotel, where she was kept awake by noise in the corridors, missed the refreshing shade of her own trees at home, and was more tired at the end of the season than at the beginning.

Mrs. Morris had to enlarge her house by a music-room and a library, because her neighbors did. She read little, but a library was a good thing to have. It made one seem intellectual. She was somewhat intelligent, but superficial. As for music, she did not play much; but sometimes her guests did, and a music-room was an attraction.

Mrs. Morris had to have a good pew in church, for she desired to be eminently respectable. She had to give occasionally, or be thought mean. She must be seen now and then at concerts, operas, and lectures, or she would not be in good society.

She had to have a horse and carriage, as these were needed for making calls. She was obliged to keep servants, because she was so busy with social life. Had her visits been among the poor or the unfortunate, they might have helped the world; but her time now was spent simply for her own social pleasure, and with the thought, perhaps, that she was adding to Mr. Morris's popularity. He cared for his home, however, far more than for the outside world, and would have been happier had he been permitted to enjoy it.

Mrs. Morris, by persistent effort and tact, had become quite a social leader. It never seemed to occur to her that, when people lived beyond their means, there must sometime be a settlement.

This came one day when Mr. Morris was severely injured by a street-car, lingered for several months, and then died. It was a great blow to Mrs. Morris in more ways than one. When the income ceased the house was sold to pay borrowed money, the parties and suppers were over, the fine clothes disappeared, and with them Mrs. Morris's position in society. The world forgot her. It was a hard lesson to learn, but a lesson that many women have learned to their sorrow. Yet many must travel the old road of experience.

TWO AT ONCE

IT WAS the afternoon of May 15. A young lady sat by an open window looking out upon the hawthorn and laburnum trees, and yet her thoughts seemed to be elsewhere.

About her was every luxury. The brick house, in Queen Anne style, was set in the midst of trees, many of them now in blossom, or graceful with their seed-tassels. Far away in the distance the ocean could be seen. The girl herself added much to this charm of the picture, as she rested her elbow upon her blue-velvet writing-desk, where scores of addressed envelopes were piled up. She took up one and read the superscription—"Herbert Underwood, 7 Brompton Place."

"I am really sorry. I wish it had not gone so far," she said aloud, as the color faded a little from her cheek; "but then," and the color came back, "Herbert will not mind it more than other men. They seem to forget such things soon. I have loved him for years, as two may who grow up together, but other girls are ready to accept him.

"I wonder if he will really care much. He will be surprised when he reads these cards announcing my marriage to another. Engaged to two at once! I suppose they will say I am a coquette. It is so delightful to be admired—to be loved. I really wish I had told him that Robert loves me also. Robert is not richer nor handsomer, but Herbert seems more like a brother.

"Besides, it will be so charming to live in Washington, and meet all the celebrities. I hope it is not frivolous, for I suppose all girls like society. I wonder what Herbert will do. Perhaps he will write me that he is broken-hearted; perhaps he will come in person and rebuke me. He is very proud, though, and I think he will bear it bravely. I had a friend who engaged herself to two at once, and the rejected young man shot himself. I hope Herbert will not do that!"

The cards were sent, and preparations went forward for a grand wedding. Dresses were tried on, and boxes of presents were opened with eager curiosity—those offerings which usually mean so little, and cramp the recipients for the next ten years in returning like favors. There was nothing from Herbert—not even a letter.

"How strange!" said the expectant bride. When Mr. Underwood received the cards he was indeed confounded, not heart-broken, for though he had long loved Clara Rawley he had questioned for some time her complete devotion to him.

She had been a society prize—rich, pretty, admired. He, likewise of fine family, could have won many. It was of course a disappointment, a humiliation. His friends would know it, and wonder at it. Some men would have taken a hasty departure to Europe; some would have been embittered by a young woman's double dealing. He determined, perhaps not the most honorable thing for him, to recompense evil for evil.

By wise investigation he ascertained at what hour the happy bridegroom, Robert Spalding, was expected at the home of his betrothed, and decided to meet him on the train previous to his arrival. They had met each other once or twice, and thus it was not difficult to discern in the crowded cars the handsome face of his rival.

"Mr. Spalding, I believe."

"Yes. Oh, I remember you—Mr. Underwood, the friend of Miss Rawley! Glad to see you; sit down."

Presently the conversation turned upon the approaching wedding, and then with apparent calmness, but with indignation, Herbert told him how he had been engaged to Miss Rawley for several years, and of her perfidy.

Mr. Spalding listened with astonishment, and when he had finished, lost faith, ceased to find her the ideal of his life. She had been faithless to one; she might be to another. She certainly was undeserving of the love he had given her. He determined, then and there, to retrace his steps, and sent her a telegram, followed by a letter, telling her of the withdrawal of his hand.

The Rawley family were in consternation when the letter was received. Clara was piqued, angered, and became ill over it, and was sent to Europe. The careless if not heartless girl had been punished.

THE HOUSE-WARMING

"ALMOST ready for the great event," said Mr. Josiah Midland, portly and genial, to his wife Martha, as they stood on the porch of a two-story brick house, nearly completed. "I want the new house for you, Martha, and I want it also, I must confess, to show the people of Collinston that Josiah Midland has been a financial success. You know life has been a struggle since I left this town a boy, and worked my way on the railroad to a place of trust. Life is not an easy thing for the best of us, and where the one gains in the race, the many are so bound by the needs of every day that they can never rise above their surroundings. I kept good habits and saved my money. I owe that teaching to my hard-working mother."

"Yes, you have been a great success," said the thin and careworn wife, who had shared his struggles and did not possess his buoyant temperament to throw off the wear of daily life. "I almost dread to have a house-warming, for it will cost so much and bring no end of work. I should like to have the people see our beautiful home, but you know I cannot shine in society."

Mrs. Midland looked up to her husband as the great factor in their worldly gains, and so he was; but he owed much to the economy and good sense of the quiet woman who was glad to be his helper.

"Oh, you will shine enough, Martha, so that I shall be proud of you! After the furniture is once in the house we will invite everybody—yes, everybody, rich and poor. It's great folly for a man to make social distinctions for himself as soon as he has a few thousands. I want to have them all enjoy the house. It's the handsomest house in the village, and they'll all be glad to come. The caterer will provide the supper, and you'll just have to shake hands with the guests and look pleased."

"What do you think I had better wear, Josiah?"

"Oh, you must have a new dress for the occasion! I like garnet. Get a garnet silk with a good deal of velvet, and you'll look handsome;" and Mr. Midland smiled in his big-hearted way that had won him friends from his boyhood.

The new moon had risen in the west, and the stars were coming out brightly, as if all nature even was glad at Mr. Midland's success. As they left the house the church bell rang out.

"Let us go," said Mr. Midland. "The minister told me the other day that an evangelist was coming here. I forgot all about it, but it might pay us to go and hear him once. Religion isn't a thing of emotion to me, but I like to hear good preaching. I've never had any notion of joining a church myself, but I don't know what the community would be without the churches. Property would go down pretty quickly."

The minister, as was human, felt the blood quicken in his veins as the successful railroad-man and his wife entered. Not that they were more important than poor people, but he knew that money consecrated to good ends is a power almost unlimited. He could only silently pray that some word would be uttered which would touch Mr. Midland's heart.

The young evangelist preached not an extraordinary sermon, but a simple talk upon the power of a good life—a life that came but once and was spent so quickly. Mr. Midland sat like one awakened out of sleep. True, he had made money; he had a good moral character; but he would go through life but once, and he was living entirely for himself. He had never realized what a wonderful gift from heaven this life is, with all its possibilities to help others, to make the poor comfortable, the sad happy, to remove the causes of crime and discontent. He seemed, all at once, to have made a voyage of discovery, and to have found a new land.

He said little on the way home, except to tell Martha that he felt strangely, and that she must go to bed and sleep, but he would sit up awhile and think. Mr. Midland did think long and carefully by the shaded lamp. He thought over his whole past experience. He had been prospered, and he owed all to a Higher Power. And after he had thought, he prayed.

In the morning he said: "Martha, I have given up the house-warming. I have decided to use the money to send a boy to college to become a preacher;" and then he added, "for a man who turns the life of another heavenward does the greatest work in the world, and I must help to do the greatest hereafter."

Mrs. Midland looked confused for a minute, and then she said, half audibly, "I am very glad, Josiah." After that night Mr. Midland's face took on an expression that was noted till his death, years afterward. It was as though he had talked with the angels, and joined a new brotherhood. The genial man became more genial, more considerate, more self-controlled. It became literally true that, like his Master, "he went about doing good." Without children of his own, he devoted his property to the giving of the Gospel to the people. He joined heartily, by voice and money, in all that elevated

49

mankind. He built houses for the poor; he educated orphans; he held prayer-meetings in sparsely-settled districts; he labored for temperance; he became the idol and ideal man of the community. He carried out his plan of using the house-warming money to educate a young man for the ministry, and lived to see his gift return a thousand-fold interest.

HANNAH AND JOE

IN THE YEAR 1851 Captain Budington, of Groton, Conn., passed the winter in Cumberland inlet, west of Greenland. Here he met Joe and Hannah on the island of Kim-ick-su-ic, so called because its flat centre, covered with grass, resembles a dogskin. Hannah was twelve years old, dressed in fur pantaloons and short fur overdress, and bore the name of Too-koo-li-too in her own language. Joe was a good deal older, and his real name was Ebierbing.

A few years afterward a merchant from Hull, England, Mr. Bolby, met them at Cumberland gulf, where they had come off the island to trade, and prevailed upon them to take the long journey to England. When he reached home he made a large company, and in the presence of these guests the young woman Hannah was married to Joe. Mr. Bolby took them to several places in England and Scotland, and they were finally presented to Queen Victoria and Prince Albert. The Queen was deeply interested in these people from the far North in British America, and asked them to dine with her. If the Queen was pleased with the sincere, uneducated, fur-dressed pair, Hannah was no less pleased with the gracious Queen in her elegant home, so entirely different from a snow hut. She always said Victoria was "very kind, very much lady." After two years they returned to Cumberland inlet, and in 1860 Charles F. Hall, the explorer, met them.

Everybody in both England and America had become deeply interested in the fate of Sir John Franklin. He had left England in 1845 with two ships, the "Erebus" and "Terror," with one hundred and thirty-four persons, in search of the North Pole. After two years relief parties were sent out to find them. Lady Franklin spent all her large fortune in sending out ships to search for her missing husband.

Finally, in 1850, the graves of three of the men were found at the far North, on Beechy island, west of Hannah's home, so that the course which Franklin took was known. Four years later Dr. Rae, of England, heard from the Eskimos that a large company of white men had starved on King William Land, far to the northwest of Baffin's bay, and he obtained from the Eskimos many articles which belonged to Franklin and his men.

After England had spent over five million dollars in searching for Franklin it was ascertained that both his ships had gone to pieces in the ice off the west coast of King William Land, and that his poor men had starved and frozen, as they wandered over the ice in a vain search for food or friends. Then skeletons were found in boats or in snowbanks, and their boots, watches, and silver had become the property of the Eskimos. Sir John died two years after the ships left England, and must have been buried in the ocean.

Some persons believed that the Franklin party were not all dead. Charles Francis Hall was an engraver at Cincinnati, O. He was poor, and with no influential friends, but he felt that the Lord had called him to the work of finding some of the Franklin men. He read all he could find about Arctic life. He asked money of prominent men and learned societies, and finally, after enough obstacles to discourage any other man, obtained funds to build a boat and put up twelve hundred pounds of food for the journey. A New London firm gave him a free passage on one of their ships, and he went, in 1860, to the far North, discovering relics of Sir Martin Frobisher's expedition, made three hundred years before. His boat was lost, so he had to return to America, and brought with him Joe and Hannah, who had been with him two years, and who were devotedly attached to him.

In 1864 Hall started again with Joe and Hannah, and north of Hudson bay lived five years among the Eskimos, eating their raw food and living in their igloos or snow huts. Joe, with great skill, would kill a walrus, which sometimes weighs two thousand pounds, or would watch two whole nights near a hole in the ice where the seal comes up to breathe, that he might spear it for his master.

In 1866, May 14, the only child of Joe and Hannah died, while on one of Hall's journeys. According to custom, the distracted mother at the plain funeral carried the dead baby in a fur blanket suspended from her neck. Captain Hall put this note in the fur cap covering the head of the child: "These are the mortal remains of little King William, the only child of Ebierbing and Too-koo-li-too, the interpreters of the lost Franklin Research Expedition. God hath its soul now, and will keep it from harm."

Later, Hall visited King William Land, and brought away one hundred and twenty-five pounds of relics of Franklin and his men. Among these was a complete skeleton, proved from the filling of a tooth to be that of an officer of the ship "Erebus." Hall felt sure now that all the party were dead. Joe and Hannah came back to the States with Hall, bringing a little three-year-old girl whom they adopted. They bought her of her parents for a sled. Hannah named her Sylvia Grinnell, after the Grinnell family, celebrated for their gifts towards Arctic research, but her real name was Punna.

Captain Hall made his third voyage in the ship "Polaris" in 1871 for the North Pole, taking his devoted Joe and Hannah and little Punna. He reached a higher point in Smith sound than had been reached by any other vessel at that time, and anchored in a harbor protected by an iceberg four hundred and fifty feet long and three hundred broad, calling the place Thank God harbor. In the autumn of this year Hall died very suddenly, and his men spent two days in digging a grave only two feet deep. He was buried at eleven in the forenoon, but so dark was it in that high latitude that lanterns were carried. Poor Hannah sobbed aloud at the death of her best friend. The party on the "Polaris" determined to return, but, being caught in the ice, were obliged to abandon her and throw the provisions and clothing out on the ice-floe. In the midst of this work, in the night, the ship drifted away, with fourteen persons on board, leaving on a piece of ice one hundred yards long and seventy-five broad Captain Tyson and eight white men and nine Eskimos, including three women and a baby eight weeks old. Hannah and Punna were among them.

A dreadful snow-storm came on, and the shivering creatures huddled together under some musk-ox skins. Later they built a little house from materials thrown out of the ship, and floated down Baffin's bay and Davis strait, the ice constantly crumbling and the sea washing over them. They used all their boats save one for fuel, and were only kept alive through the heroic efforts of Joe and another Eskimo, Hans, who caught some seals for them, which were eagerly eaten uncooked, without removing the hairy skin. They had only a little mouldy bread, and the sufferings of the children from hunger were painful to witness.

Once, when nearly all were dead from starvation, Joe saved them by killing a bear. He and Hannah refused to leave Captain Tyson and the party when they were drifting past their homes at Cumberland inlet, even when it was probable that the Eskimos themselves must be used for food by the famished white men. After drifting one thousand five hundred miles in six months (one hundred and ninety-six days), one of the most thrilling journeys on record, the party were rescued off the coast of Labrador by the English ship "Tigress."

Hannah and Joe settled at Groton in 1873, in a little house purchased for them by their good friend, "Father Hall." Joe became a carpenter, and Hannah made up furs and other articles on her sewing-machine.

The next year Hannah, at the age of thirty-eight, died of consumption, her health broken by the exposure on the ice-floe. She had long been an earnest Christian, loving and reading her Bible daily. She was tenderly cared for by Mrs. Captain Budington and others, saying at the last, "Come, Lord Jesus, and take thy poor creature home!" A handsome stone marks the grave of the faithful Hannah in the cemetery. Joe came often to the graves on the hillside of Groton, and said at last, "Hannah gone! Punna gone! Me go now again to King William Land; I have to fight; me no care." He went with Lieutenant Schwatka in the Franklin search party, June 19, 1878, and never returned to the United States.

54

BURTON CONE'S REASON

YEARS after Coleridge wrote the beautiful "Hymn before Sunrise in the Valley of Chamouni," which Felicia Hemans said she would give all her poems to have written,—among a group of strangers standing in awe before Mont Blanc was a man who seemed forty-five, from his hair fully half gray and his quiet, dignified bearing, though he must have been younger. He was absorbed in his own thoughts. He did not look at any face about him, but seemed spell-bound by the sublimity of the scene. In that vast mountain, white with eternal snows, with the rivers, fed by the glaciers, turbulent at its base, the sun clothing it with rainbows, he saw the same God who had compassed his life, as the stalwart pines hedged in the grand mount before him.

After a time, as through that as yet undeveloped science of unseen power between mind and mind, he felt a presence. He was conscious of eyes fixed upon him, conscious that somebody he had known and loved was near him. A hand was laid on his shoulder.

"Burton, you're the last man in all the world I thought of seeing. Ten years since you and I travelled together, and you yet on the wing? I supposed you had settled down to some life-work, and was surrounded by loves and cares ere this. You and I have stood here together before."

The speaker was a genial, generous man, somewhat Cone's junior in look and manner, whose sorrows, whether many and great or not, could not long crush his happy heart. His sympathies were quick, his hopes naturally bright, and his nature ardent. The decade that had passed since the former companionship had aged one more than the other. The one had been giving time and heart to business, but had lived alone, though a crowded world was about him. The other had been kept young and fresh by the love of a cheerful wife and sunny daughter, and the years had gone by rapidly and more than ordinarily well stored with good deeds.

"Come, Burton, I am tiring of this road and grandeur. Let's go back to the hotel and have one of the old friendly talks. Nature has lost half its beauty now that only one pair of eyes sees it—and I have no one to tell of the beautiful or strange things I have seen. You don't need friendship as I do. You are made of sterner stuff. You are Mont Blanc personified."

Cone's mind was full of the grandeur before him, but his

55

heart, cold as he was, was keenly alive to the needs of those who had been friends, so together they walked arm in arm to their lodgings.

"Now, let's talk over the ten years, Cone. Ten years make a fool or a wise man of a fellow—carry him up to the gates or down to the depths."

"Tell me what they have done for you, Marsh. You know how much I have to thank you and your young wife for the sunshine you put into my life when we travelled together before. She seemed like a sister to me. She understood me; and that is where most women fail. They do not know us, or we do not know them, so our true natures never come side by side; but she seemed to feel the pulse of my life. She knew just when I needed jovial words and when I needed sympathy or quiet. She had the tact I have heard so often described, but seldom seen, and a pure, good heart back of it. I fear all hasn't gone right with you. Can it be that you are walking alone, like myself?"

Tears gathered in Marsh's eyes. He had almost a woman's heart and a woman's love. "It isn't hard for you to stand alone, but for me it is crushing. I buried my wife in England six months ago. We came for her health, but she failed rapidly and went away soon after we arrived. Our little girl is boarding with friends, and I wander anywhere, everywhere,—so I can forget. I cannot go back to America. Nothing binds me there. I seem unfit for labor, and I am adrift. You know she was like an anchor. I depended upon her judgment, upon her help, upon her love. When a woman leans entirely upon a man, and she is taken away, he may feel as though something dear and beautiful had gone out from him; but when a woman has strength enough to be a companion, a counsellor, in the deeds and plans of every day,—when she is not a pet merely, but a guide to everything noble,—when, whether you will or not, you are kept upon a plane of right and duty and manhood,—what shall a poor relying heart do?"

"Would you wish to forget, Marsh? I would put such a blessing away in my heart and grow strong from daily looking at it."

"I can't keep it, Cone. I must get away from such memories. I feel as though I drifted hither and thither, because there is no hand on the helm. To remember is misery: to forget might be relief."

"And yet, do you not owe such a wife a loving, yearning remembrance? One might forget a flower that blossomed for his pleasure for a day or a week; but hold in grateful memory a spring that opened in the desert of a parched life and became an unfailing supply. Memories sometimes are almost as sweet as present

56

realities, and sometimes we are made even stronger by the one than by the other."

"That may be good philosophy for those who have never loved and lost. No one can know till he has the trial. I have one left, I know, but that does not fill the place of the other, and perchance no one ever could."

"You must go back with me to our fatherland. I am nearly through my journeying, for it seems idle work for me now. Besides, I have had premonitions that I should make ready for another journey. You seem startled. Ten years have worn upon me, for they have been years of constant and hard labor. I could not forget, and would not; but hope will fade into fruition by and by."

"Cone, you ought to tell me of your life. Much as you respected my wife, you never raised the curtain from the scenes which transpired before we met you. Why have you lived to your age, and taken no heart into your own to bless and hold? Your principles are like adamant, and would keep you anywhere, but every man and woman needs to have his or her heart uncloistered, that others may grow strong and unselfish with him. This working out life's plan alone, with no giving or receiving of loves, seems a mistake to me. Has your heart anything hidden away in it, or are you proof to what you may think the weaker acts of life?"

Cone's face seemed a little troubled. Not one man or woman out of ten thousand reaches the age of forty without having loved or been loved, and felt blessed joy or bitter pain in one or the other. Was he indeed different from the rest of mankind? He manifested no partiality for women, except a deference that everybody pays to what it supposes exalted and ennobling. He had received numerous proofs of their esteem for him, and indications that they would not repel his attentions. He was often the subject of remark, from his striking face and manner, but when all the queries had been asked and unanswered they said, "There must be a reason for all this, and time will tell it."

He had been touched in heart by Marsh's utter helplessness. He knew better than anybody else what a centre she had been to his thought and his affections. He sympathized with him. Perhaps the doors of his own inner sanctuary, locked for a half-score years, might swing back just once, and let a weary friend come in and find consolation.

"Come to-night, Marsh, and I will talk with you. Good-by till then."

Alone and unperceived he stole out to sit under the majestic shadows of Mont Blanc, and worship. Nobody with a God in his heart ever stands there without holding communion with Him. No wonder that the lofty peaks, echoing cañons, and wondrous waterfalls of our own country have written the names of more than one poet on the pages of American literature! Such scenes are the nurseries in which great minds develop. Such grand handiwork of the Builder draws every man very near to Him.

Burton Cone had never forgotten the scenes through which he had passed. Though some things had been laid away and sealed with the seal of silence for over a dozen years, they were fresh to him as though they had taken place that very morning. Perhaps he did not need sympathy as some need it; perhaps he did not wish to burden others with his feelings.

It seemed almost twilight in the room, the lights were turned down so low.

"Sit down, Marsh, till we talk of the past. You have wondered if there is anything back of this life you have known. Aye, much, very much! You have wondered if I ever loved, and why I did not love some one now, when I so reverence woman. Away back in New England, in a little town near a beautiful city on the Connecticut, is the home of my childhood. That is precious to me, though I have not seen it for years. Near it is a large brick house, painted white, with long rows of firs and pines leading to it. It looks like an old castle. In that home was a young girl who from her childhood was my ideal. We played together as children, we roamed through the woods and meadows, we read and sang and talked of things beyond our years, because her nature held me above myself. She was not beautiful to others, perchance; but to me her large dark eyes, high brow, and glossy hair, with her quiet, dignified manner, made her a queen. She never seemed to do wrong. She had to ask no one's forgiveness. She never made mistakes. She had no need for regrets. Nobody thought to be rude or rough to Mary Fairchild, or in her presence. She was always calm, always genial and kind, always considerate. She never seemed like the rest of us. I fancied she had been sent from heaven to keep our earthly minds and tastes somewhat akin to theirs. I always feared she might at any time take her departure to the land where she seemed rightly to belong.

"She went away to receive her education, and I studied hard to make myself, if possible, some day worthy of her. Occasionally she wrote me, and those letters seemed to me of peculiar value. I read each one over and over again, till I knew every word and how every letter was made. The slightest allusion to friendship for me seemed

58

a mine of joy, and I put the letter next my heart to read as often as I should get a little leisure. She never gave me encouragement that she loved me more than others, always treating us all in the same gracious, kindly way. I was naturally timid, and though I did not tell her I loved her my desire to be in her company, my extreme joy when I met her, my blushing cheeks and my glad eyes, must have told her over and over again that I idolized her. I was active, energetic, ardent, but I lacked her spirituality and finer qualities of soul. She revelled in all that was beautiful and artistic. I never expected that she could love me as I did her. I thought her nature too ethereal, but I hoped that I might sometime live in her presence and be guided by her blessed spirit in my daily life.

"Nothing could have been farther removed from coarseness or passion than my love for Mary; I never pressed my lips to hers. So I could be near her, hear her voice, and live in the sunshine of herself, I was content. I went out from her society a better man each time. I would go any distance, endure any exposure, so I might but feel the blessed light of her eyes come into mine. I never joked with her as I might others. I never used her name before any person. I never wrote it carelessly. Everything pertaining to her was sacred as the heaven which I sometime expected to enter. My highest thought was her happiness, not mine. My ambition, my hopes, my prayers, all centred in that one desire to walk beside her in the beautiful journey of life. When any person coupled my name with hers in pleasantry I felt as though they had touched a name that was hallowed, and changed the subject. I longed to be constantly in her presence, yet dared not trouble her too much; so between desire to hover near and fear of being an annoyance rather than a joy my soul was constantly harassed. I had often pledged myself to ask her to accept my homage, and though I had means and social position and education, everything seemed unworthy of her. What if she refused to be my guide forever? Life then would be worse than useless; so, hoping and praying, I waited, and my worship grew as the months went by. Every flower that she loved I pressed and laid away in the books I had seen her read. Every kindly word she gave me made me joyful for days. Every touch of her hand thrilled me with delight, and I lived over the bliss a thousand times in memory. Once, I remember, when I gave her a picture of myself, and she looked at it long and earnestly I thought, and her dark hair touched mine, I was too happy for words to express it.

"Other young men called upon her, and, like myself, showed her the deference that belonged to a pure, beautiful woman, girl though she was in years. Among them was a noble young man, the perfection of manly grace and the embodiment of manly virtues. Alfred Trumbull was a preacher, a genial, earnest, eloquent young man, as spiritual as herself. I had met him there and had learned to love him. He admired her, we all plainly saw, but she treated him as the rest, with a cordiality that was blended with reserve and that kept us all removed just far enough to worship her.

"Weeks went by. I was growing wretched. I was coming to know how entirely dependent I was upon her for happiness. If a day passed by and I did not see her, it was a lost day. I must tell her and have her all my own. Oh, Marsh, those were glad days, after all,—when I could see her, if no more,—but God and time shape things differently from what we will!

"It was just such a night as this. I remember her so plainly—how I stood by the gate and watched the shadows of the pines flicker on the walk, and, man though I was, trembled to take the final step. She met me so cordially, more than was her wont, I thought. She was so lovely on that calm summer evening; so doubly frail, too, that my solicitude for her kept pace with my love. She was alone. With no sound save the rustle of the pines, and no one to hear save God and her, I told her all my heart. I told her how I worshipped her with all the strength of my being. I told her how I would struggle to the end of life to make myself worthy of her.

"She waited a full minute before she answered me. In that minute it seemed as though my reason would give way. She was so white with the moonlight streaming in upon her, as she put her hand in mine and said, with an irrepressible tenderness, 'Burton' (and nobody else spoke my name as she did), 'Burton, I have promised to help Alfred Trumbull win souls.'

At first I was dumb; then I buried my face in my hands and groaned aloud, then I wept like a child that cannot be comforted. Oh, Marsh, there is nothing that bends a man's soul like that! I felt alone—no support, no guide, no love, no hope. Life was worse than a blank; a dull, dread certainty of sorrow. It would be torture to die if death were to remove me from her sight—it would be torture to live and never have her love or presence. Those were bitter days, full of the depths of sorrow. Those days made me grow old a score of years. I was never young afterward.

"At last, when I could command myself, I begged to be allowed to love her till my life went out. If any one could win her instead of me, I was thankful to have it one so good as Alfred Trumbull. I conquered self. I found my highest happiness was still to see her happy. Sometimes when I visited her the old love, the yearning to claim her for myself, would sweep over me till my head grew dizzy and my heart sank within me, and then my better nature said: 'Rejoice in her joy, and be content only to love.'

"I came at last to be resigned—yes, happy in my idol-worship. From her I could hope for nothing but kindness and tenderness, but I could never love any other. The time drew near when she and Alfred Trumbull were to commence their grand life-work. Suddenly his health failed. She went to him—she cared for him day and night with the same intensity of love that I had given her. It could not arrest disease. He longed for returning health, because they would have been so happy and congenial in their love and work; but one day in early spring he died in her arms, and was laid away among the first flowers, to rest from his labors.

"I never saw a life so blighted as hers. Her whole heart lay beside his in the grave. She lost all interest in life. She grew quiet and sad and more ethereal. She never mentioned his name, but we knew she longed to live with him, even though she must pass through the valley of the shadow.

"Against all my struggling I found my old desire to claim her coming back into my soul. I showed her all the delicate yet unobtrusive kindness possible. Her very sorrow made her unspeakably dear.

"After Alfred had been in heaven a year, and knowing that she loved no one else, I told her again the old burden of my heart. She seemed moved to pity as she laid her hand on mine, just as she did once before, and said in tones I shall never forget, 'Burton, I am Alfred's!'

"I lived over again the old days of torture, and again conquered self to minister to her happiness. I should have died if I could not have loved her, and I was almost happy that she did not deny me this. I gathered beautiful and rare things for her, and in all ways made her life less sad, if possible. I must have her to care for and love and serve, and again I laid my affection at her feet. With the same sad smile she had borne for three years, she said, looking down at the mourning robes she had worn for him, 'Burton, I am Alfred's still; but if I can make your life any happier I will be your wife!'

"Those words staggered me. I had not dared hope for this, though I prayed for it. Joy seemed to take away my senses; and seeing me so beside myself the old look came back once or twice to her face. I was as one who, shipwrecked in mid-ocean, after clinging

61

for days to a floating plank, at last picked up by a stray ship, is helpless through joy and gratitude. I was more dead than alive with my wealth of happiness. Mary and I were made one. Marsh, how I live over again those beautiful days. I used to look at your pretty wife beside you as we journeyed, and think of my precious Mary.

"My cup of joy was full to the brim. She accepted my homage, and was grateful. I spared no pains to make her life complete. To have her in my home, to have the blessed influence of her presence evening after evening, was the crowning joy of a man who had loved for years in silence and unreturned affection.

"I was so entranced with my joy that another summer had come round again before I began to realize that she was fully mine, and then the next winter flew so rapidly, and a little son came into the household. We were both very grateful—I all the more because I thought it might fill Mary's heart something as the old love had done.

"I watched her cheeks grow brighter as she fondled the boy, whom I named Alfred for her sake. They were so beautiful in my home, mother and child. I worked with redoubled energy, and well nigh forgot that there was any heaven beyond, my joy was so complete below.

"Spring came and I gathered wild flowers to wreathe the brows of both. One day, while absent from home, a message came for me that my wife was ill and desired me to come. I grew palsied with fear. I hastened home to find her just able to speak to me. She had had a violent hæmorrhage of the lungs. I was wild. I knelt before her, and clasping her in my arms begged her not to die, but live for my sake and her boy's. She put her white arm about my neck, drawing me to his little face and hers, as she said faintly, 'Burton, keep the darling child, who is ours,—but I—I am Alfred's!'—and was gone.

"For months I did not know what happened. All was a blank. My boy died before I came to myself, and I was alone again in the world. I travelled till my health permitted work, and then I labored incessantly.

"I love Mary now as I loved her so long ago. No other can ever fill her place. She is as much mine to love as ever. All this has whitened my hair, you see. I must lock up my heart again, lest the world look in upon my idols. Do you see that I have reason for not loving again?"

Marsh's head was bowed. He loved Cone as a brother, and he had suffered all this and loved on, and was brave and strong.

"Let us take my little girl and go back to yours and Mary's home," said Marsh.

"Yes, and Mary has an only sister strangely like your wife. You need another heart to lean upon. Your nature is different from mine."

Not many years after Marsh had taken the sister to be a mother to his pretty daughter, and Burton Cone, leaving his property to this little one, had been laid to rest by the side of Mary.

UNSUITABLE

"IT NEVER will happen," said Jane Holcomb to her sister Nancy, as they sat together before an open fire. "Justus is too bright a young man to fall in love with a woman nearly twice his own age. Think of our educating our only nephew at a most expensive college, having all our hopes centred in his future prominence, and then have him make an unsuitable marriage!"

"But we have never seen this woman he seems to love," said Nancy quietly. "Perhaps we should like her. I think she must have some admirable qualities, or Justus would never be fond of her. Besides, he is a favorite with ladies, and could marry surely a pretty girl of his own age."

Jane and Nancy Holcomb were sisters, well-to-do in the world, very necessary to each other, but not especially necessary to the rest of the community. Nancy was half an invalid, who repaid the care of her sister with a nearly perfect affection. She would have made a lovely wife had she been married some years before.

It was fortunate that Jane had never married. Her continual worry lest a particle of dust adhere to table or chair, her constant picking up of book, or shawl, or gloves, if anything were left for a moment out of place, would have made her an annoyance to any man who wished to enjoy his home. If a picture had been painted of Jane Holcomb, it would not have been complete without a broom in her hand. There was one good servant in the house who kept things reasonably neat, but Jane was forever cleaning. If she had married, and had been the mother of children, probably she would have been less fussy, and a pleasanter woman to live with.

Both women idolized the bright nephew, Justus, who loved his aunts in the abstract, but usually kept as far away from Aunt Jane's broom as possible.

He was a handsome young fellow, cheery, cordial, earnest, sympathetic, and withal possessed of excellent common-sense. He had just graduated from a medical school, and was coming home for a visit to the aunts. Jane swept and dusted more than ever, till the carpets and furniture would have protested, if that were possible. Nancy grew fresher and better in health from the expected arrival.

Finally the young man came, and was kissed and petted as young men are apt to be by women older than themselves. Aunt Jane looked him over from head to foot. Yes, he was clean and attractive, even to her practised eye.

"Now, Justus," she said, as they were sitting by the open fire after supper, "tell your aunts about the love matter which we hear of. I think this lady is a little older than you." Jane controlled herself and became diplomatic, because a young man cannot usually be driven, but must be gently led.

"If you mean Miss Watterson—yes, she is a charming woman. She is thirty-five, just ten years older than I. I confess she attracts me more than any of the girls of my own age. She is not handsome, but very intelligent, has read widely, and is a noble woman."

"But you surely would be the subject of much remark in society if you married her. And we are so proud of you, Justus, we naturally wish you could marry rich, and some one who could help you in your profession. You know a woman can help to make her husband popular or unpopular."

"I know it, aunt; but, after all, I need the right kind of companionship when I marry. I have not decided the matter yet, and perhaps I shall grow wiser."

"You must not forget also, Justus, that as a rule a woman grows old faster than a man, or she used to. I cannot say that she does exactly in this new age, when American men are killing themselves in business, and the women are living in luxury. But when you are forty-five and in your prime, your wife will be fifty-five; and the disparity will be more apparent then than now. Besides, you will see so many attractive faces in your profession."

"That would not influence me, Aunt Jane. If I loved her once, I should hope to be man enough to love her always. But I will wait awhile before I"—

"That is right," said Nancy; "you know we shall make you our heir, that is, sister Jane will, and we want you to be a leader socially and in your profession. You know men have such a wide sphere of influence. All our lives centre in you."

"Don't build too much upon my future, Aunt Nancy, though I will do my best."

"Do you correspond with Miss Watterson?" said Jane half hesitatingly.

"We have done so, but we have discontinued it, as I am sure she thinks the difference in our ages a possible obstacle to our future happiness."

"Well, she is a wise woman not to let a boy be captured even in accord with his own wishes. Why it is that young men so often like older women I'm sure I can't tell."

"Because they are natural and not simpering, feel an interest

65

and dare to show it, are vivacious without flippancy, and usually well-enough read to be companionable to an educated man. You know, Aunt Jane, a man doesn't want simply a pretty face to look on forever. He must have something besides a vine nowadays."

"Well, tell us about Miss Watterson?"

"She has travelled abroad, plays delightfully, loves to do charitable work, has tact enough to know when to talk and when to be silent, likes to look well, but does not spend all her time in dress as do some whom I know, whether their fathers can afford it or not, and doesn't seem to make any especial effort to win my affections, but is thoroughly appreciative."

"Why hasn't she married before this? Been in love and been disappointed, I warrant."

"That I don't know. She has never told me. I suppose, like yourself, Aunt Jane, she hasn't found a man good enough."

Jane Holcomb smiled in a pleased kind of way at this delicate allusion to her superior judgment.

"Well, Justus, I wish you would promise me that you won't write to Miss Watterson for one year, and by that time you will probably have found some one more suitable to your age."

"I promise, but I shall be so busy with my profession that I fear no other lady will command my time."

When Justus departed Jane kissed him with not only maternal fondness, but with that woman's pride that feels she has for once circumvented an attractive woman, doubtless in love with a bright and handsome nephew.

"One year will fix matters," she said to Nancy, after Justus had gone. "Few loves can bear such a silence as that."

"I fear Justus will be lonesome," said Nancy, who still had a little longing in her heart that the youth might have the woman of his choice, even though "unsuitable," as Jane had said. There was a touch of romance in Nancy that would have made her an interesting woman if circumstances had been permitted to develop her.

Long letters came from Justus. He was busy and successful. Jane was happy, but Nancy thought she detected a depressed feeling in the letters. He was lonely, of course. Who can enjoy the companionship of a cultivated and womanly woman and not miss it? Who that has had one sincere affection, especially if it have something of reverence in it, can readily supply its place with another?

One morning, after a year had passed, a square envelope came, and a full, kind, but decided letter. It contained cards announcing the marriage of Justus Holcomb and Miss Watterson. What society would say, what even his good aunts would say, had been weighed in the balance and been found wanting.

Jane was sadly disappointed. "Another instance of a woman's power," she said. "I never knew a woman that couldn't do what she set out to do, if a man's heart were at stake. I feared it all the while. Men will do such foolish things. I fear Justus will regret, but he is so manly he will never say so."

"But she may be better for him than a fly-away-girl," Nancy suggested. "I hope it will turn out well. We must be kind to them and write them to come to see us."

Jane set the house in order, and swept and dusted, and made herself ready for the inevitable. When the visit was made and Justus was found to be happy with a wife ten years his senior, Jane was in a measure reconciled. "It could have been worse," she said to Nancy. "She seems a very clever person."

"I like her," said Nancy; "she has a very sweet smile, and this makes even a plain face attractive. I don't believe she tried to get him, for he seems more in love than she does."

"Ah! that's a woman's skill in covering," said Jane. "But men will be foolish, I suppose, till the end of the world."

PLAYING WITH HEARTS

SEVERAL instances, showing the results of playing with hearts, have come under my notice, which have emphasized in my mind the danger of being careless in such matters.

That it is natural for young men to admire and love young women goes without saying. As well argue that we must not love flowers and music and sunlight, as to say one must not love the beauty and grace and sweetness of young womanhood.

A home to many if not most young men means all that is restful and delightful; a place for comfort after the toil of the day; a place of companionship with some one whose interests are identical with his, and whose tastes are congenial to his own. He does not wait, as does a woman, to see if love be reciprocal. He loves, and hopes for and asks for a return.

The girl is apt to be less impulsive. She, or her mother for her, is perhaps worldly wise, and considers well whether the man can support her, and whether he will probably make her happy. She accepts the attentions of one or a dozen, and decides among them. This is right according to our modern society, but she too often forgets whether she is giving pain needlessly.

It is too much the fashion to argue that men are not deeply touched in such matters; that, full of business as they are, a refusal is easily borne, and another love takes the place.

True, we read in the daily press quite often of a suicide resulting from a rebuff or a broken promise, but we seem to forget, unless perchance it touches our own home circle, and then the mother's heart breaks for her tenderly reared son or daughter.

I believe the history of the world shows that men love deeply, and with an affection as lasting as that of women. Who can ever forget the undying affection of Sir Walter Scott for fair young Margaret? He met and loved her at nineteen, and for six years worked at his law drudgery, looking forward to a happy union with her. He said to a friend, "It was a proud night with me when I first found that a pretty young woman could think it worth while to sit and talk with me hour after hour, in a corner of the ball-room, while all the world were capering in our view."

As his first year's practice brought him but $125, his second $290, and his third $420, the young lady counselled waiting for better days.

Two years later Margaret was married to the eldest son of a baronet, afterward Sir William Forbes, and died thirteen years after her marriage. The cause of her change of mind is not known.

At first Scott felt that he had been wronged, but this feeling against Margaret soon subsided, and was replaced by an unchangeable affection. She became the heroine of "Rokeby" and of "Woodstock."

Thirty years later, when Europe and America were filled with praise of Scott, he met the mother of his early love. He writes in his diary, after the meeting:

"I went to make a visit, and fairly softened myself like an old fool, with recalling old stories till I was fit for nothing but shedding tears and repeating verses for the whole night. This is sad work. The very grave gives up its dead, and time rolls back thirty years to add to my perplexities. I don't care. I begin to grow case-hardened, and, like a stag turning at bay, my naturally good temper grows fierce and dangerous. Yet what a romance to tell, and told, I fear, it will one day be. And then my three years of dreaming and my two years of awakening will be chronicled, doubtless. But the dead will feel no pain."

When he visited St. Andrews he recalled how thirty-four years before he had carved her name in runic characters on the turf beside the castle gate, and asked himself why, at fifty-six, that name "should still agitate his heart."

I never read of stern and fearless Andrew Jackson without recalling his devoted love for Rachel Robards. With the world he was thought to be domineering and harsh, and was often profane; but with her he was patient, gentle, and deferential. Having no children, they adopted her nephew when but a few days old. When Jackson conquered at New Orleans and young ladies strewed flowers along the path of the hero, to have the commendation of Rachel was more than that of all the world beside. When he was elected President she said, "Well, for Mr. Jackson's sake I am glad; for my own part I never wished it."

Earnest in her religious convictions, he built a small brick church for her in the Hermitage grounds, that she might gather her neighbors and servants about her for worship. Mrs. Jackson died suddenly just after her husband's election to the presidency. He could not believe that she was dead. When they brought a table to lay her body upon, "Spread four blankets upon it. If she does come to, she will lie so hard upon the table."

All night long he sat beside the form of his beloved Rachel, often feeling of her heart and pulse. In the morning he was wholly inconsolable, and when he found that she was really dead the body could scarcely be forced from his arms. He prepared a tomb for her like an open summer-house, and buried her under the white dome supported by marble pillars.

While Jackson lived he wore her miniature constantly about his neck, and every night laid it open beside her prayer-book at his bedside. Her face was the last thing upon which his eyes rested before he slept, and the first thing upon which his eyes opened in the morning, through those eight years at the White House. He made his will bequeathing all his property to his adopted son, because, said he, "If she were alive she would wish him to have it all, and to me her wish is law."

Two days before he died he said, "Heaven will be no heaven to me if I do not find my wife there." He used to say, "All I have achieved—fame, power, everything—would I exchange, if she could be restored to me for a moment."

Washington Irving cherished forever the memory of Matilda Hoffman, who died at the age of seventeen. He could never hear her name mentioned afterward. After his death a package was found marked "Private Mems." In a faded manuscript of his own writing were a lovely miniature of Matilda and a braid of fair hair. For years Irving kept her Bible and prayer-book under his pillow, and to the end of his life these were always carried with him on his journeys.

In the faded manuscript one reads:

"The ills that I have undergone in this life have been dealt out to me drop by drop, and I have tasted all their bitterness. I saw her fade rapidly away: beautiful and more beautiful, and most angelical to the last.

"I seemed to care for nothing; the world was a blank to me. I abandoned all thought of the law. I went into the country, but could not bear the solitude, yet could not endure society.... I seemed to drift about without aim or object, at the mercy of every breeze; my heart wanted anchorage. I was naturally susceptible, and tried to form other attachments, but my heart would not hold on; it would continually recur to what it had lost; and whenever there was a pause in the hurry of novelty and excitement I would sink into dismal dejection. For years I could not talk on the subject of this hopeless regret; I could not even mention her name; but her image was continually before me, and I dreamed of her incessantly."

"For time makes all but true love old;
The burning thoughts that then were told

70

Run molten still in memory's mould,
And will not cool
Until the heart itself is cold
In Lethe's pool."

The memory of Ann Rutledge never faded from the heart of Abraham Lincoln. Years after her death he was heard to say, "My heart lies buried in the grave of that girl. I can never be reconciled to have the snow, rains, and storms beat upon her grave."

Gruff Samuel Johnson worked in his garret, a most inconvenient room, after his "Tetty" died, because, said he, "In that room I never saw Mrs. Johnson." Her wedding-ring was placed in a little box, and tenderly kept till his death.

Michael Angelo's devotion to Vittoria Colonna will be told, perhaps, even after the wonderful statues of Day and Night are lost or destroyed. "He bore such a love to her," said his pupil Condivi "that I remember to have heard him say that he grieved at nothing so much as that when he went to see her pass from this life he had not kissed her brow or her face, as he kissed her hand. After her death he frequently stood trembling and as if insensible."

All lovers of art know of Saskia, whose life was to Rembrandt like the transcendent light he threw over his pictures; whose death left him forever in the shadow of shadows.

If men give such affection as these men gave,—and tens of thousands do,—then the affection is worth the most careful consideration; accepted, if possible, with gratitude that one has been thought worthy of homage; refused, if necessary, with the utmost delicacy and kindness.

Young women sometimes, perhaps because of youth, do not realize the far-reaching influence of what the world is pleased to jest about as "love affairs."

An acquaintance of mine, pretty, intelligent, and reared by a Christian mother, became engaged to two young men at the same time. One of course was refused, with, to him, bitter heartache. She married the other, led a wretched life with him, and finally was divorced.

Another received for years the attention of a worthy and wealthy young man. Another young man visited her, for whom she possibly had a preference. Both offered themselves to her, and both were accepted, she doubtless hoping to choose later the one who pleased her best. Both discovered her plan, were indignant, and left her to make other conquests.

71

These cases are far from isolated. I do not believe they arise from the heartlessness of women, but from lack of thought and care. A man can offer a woman nothing higher than a sincere love. While she need not assume that men who offer her attention wish to marry her, it is a mistake to keep one's eyes shut, and open them only to find that a heart has been hurt temporarily, and perchance permanently. Good common-sense as well as principle are necessary in matters pertaining to hearts.

DUTY

"JAMES, I hear you are getting interested in Martha Wenham!" said good old Mrs. Matthews, tremblingly, to her only son, as they sat by the fire one evening after he had returned from a hard day's work.

He had been her only support for four years, ever since her kind husband died. His sister Nellie, sweet but fragile, had leaned upon his strong arm for help, for she was unable to support herself.

Mrs. Clayton, a neighbor, had been over telling James's mother what she had heard about the young people: that they had been seen to walk very leisurely home from singing-schools and prayer-meetings, and that, at the last church picnic, he and Martha, regardless of all the others, had sauntered off to a cool, cosey nook, and were seemingly very happy and very much absorbed, as people are wont to be under such circumstances. Martha was a very excellent girl, the daughter of a well-to-do village merchant, would make one of the best of wives, and James would be fortunate to win her; but poor Mrs. Matthews saw herself and Nellie cast upon the world, for in case James married he could no more than support his wife and the little ones that would probably be born to them. He had been a faithful son, leaving school and books that he loved, to work with his hands and earn his bread. He had been able to pay their rent, get them a few neat clothes, and buy all necessary food.

Sometimes he seemed rather quiet, as though he longed again for the school days, that he might realize his ambition to be a prominent man in the world. When either mother or daughter caught a glimpse of any such feelings, they tried to make the home pleasanter for him. Mrs. Matthews baked things he liked, and Nellie took a little picture from her scantily furnished room to hang in his, or gathered a few flowers for his table.

No wonder the dependent mother spoke anxiously about his interest in Martha Wenham.

"Yes, I like her very much, mother. I think she is the noblest girl I ever saw!"

Mrs. Matthews trembled more and more. She wanted to ask him if he ever thought of marrying her, but she could not.

Finally, after long silence, James said, as though he had been weighing the thing in his own mind, "Do you think she would make me a good wife, mother?"

73

"I—I think she might, James, but what would your poor mother do?" and the tears gathered in her eyes. "I'm afraid I'm a burden, James! Don't you wish there were no obstacles in the way? Oh, James, I wonder God arranged it so!" and the fond mother could have longed to be out of the way, that her boy's happiness might be completed.

James Matthews's big heart was full. He had never thought of leaving his mother, and, though he loved Martha, duty was first with him always; so he put his hard hands upon his mother's gray head and kissed her, bidding her not to fear; that he should never leave her, and that she was better than all the Marthas in the world, and as for Nellie, he'd work his fingers off for her before any other girl should take her place.

That night there was a timid knock at Martha's door, and James Matthews was cordially welcomed. Several times before all the commonplaces were talked of he tried to tell her his errand in coming, but his courage as often failed. Martha broke the ice for him when she said, "I think, James, that day spent at the picnic was the pleasantest of my life." What could be more delightful than to hear from her own lips the very confession he had longed to hear—that his presence was a pleasure to her, that she perhaps in some measure returned his affection?

"It was a very happy one to me," responded James. "I have often wondered if it gave you pleasure. Martha, perhaps you do not know that I have loved you for a long time, and perhaps it is wrong for me to tell you of it, seeing that I cannot marry anybody."

"And why not?" said Martha, a blush spreading over her fair face and losing itself in her golden hair.

"Because my mother and sister are dependent upon me, and as long as they live—and I hope it may be many years—I shall take care of them. I could love you always without marriage, but that is the only bond that can keep you mine alone and forever. Others will be seeking one so good as you are. I could not ask you to be engaged, for you might wait for years before I was able to support a third in our home, and support you as nicely as I should wish to do. You have had too many comforts to receive poverty at my hands."

"You know I am young, James, only seventeen, and I can wait a great many years for you. I love you very much, and I have a good home to wait in; so what matter, so long as we are near each other? I'll wait until I'm an old lady, James, if need be."

The noble girl had answered as her pure heart had prompted.

Many a man knows how rich, and happy, and satisfied James Matthews felt that night as he came home in the moonlight. How

74

strong his arms felt for work, and how strong his good principles seemed!

He could do anything now for mother and sister—make any sacrifice; for did not one wait for him whose encouragement was more than money, to live with whom for one year even would recompense for a score of years of labor?

Mrs. Matthews and Nellie grew happier as they saw him so cheerful, and as his wages increased with his larger experience, and more of the comforts of life were obtained, Nellie, with less anxiety and more ease, grew better.

Two years had passed, and changes had come to Martha Wenham. Her father was dead, his property gone, and her health impaired by long and weary care of him. What was left for her but to claim the hand of him for whom she had waited these two years? Refusing all others, she had been true to him. Now came the time of trial to both.

Martha was helpless, and had nowhere to look but to him. His heart clung to her now more than ever, but who could support the two who seemed to be left providentially on his hands? Many an evening he passed with her, feeling every time as though the day of parting, if it must come to that, would be unbearable; finally he resolved to marry her, take her to his home, and do all in his power for the three. It could be only a scanty subsistence he could earn for them, and by taking another upon himself, would he not spoil the happiness of them all? He might have but one meal a day for himself, and he was willing; but what poor reward for the girl who had lost so many good places in life to share penury with him!

"James, I have a plan to propose to you, though you may not second it, and indeed I do not know if it be right or best," said Martha to him one night. "William Stillson, you know, has loved me from the time we were children together, and has always been a warm friend to me, even after I refused him. In these days of anxiety and prospective want, he has offered me again himself and his lovely home. I respect him, James, but you have my heart and he knows it. All rests with you. Shall I marry him, and thus free you from what must necessarily be a burden?"

James could not answer, and when she put her cheek upon his and held his hand, he said, "Oh, Martha, I cannot give you up!"

"My will is yours," she said, and kissed him good-night.

It troubled him after he came home. She might be so comfortable with William, so cramped with him. His duty was plain before him. He took a pen and paper and hastily wrote:

75

My Martha: I release you! I know what is best for you! Marry William and be happy. There is no other course. I shall be happy because you are. My blessing go with you.

Your
James.

Four weeks after, Martha, a woman through her sufferings, and true to her womanhood in acting honestly, gave her hand to William Stillson, promising to be his faithful wife. James heard the words that separated them forever, and seemed to grow stronger for his duties at home. He never visited her, but when she bore a beautiful boy to her husband, he felt that he might love the child, and this wee one became his plaything for many a month, until they moved to a distant part of the country. Then, for the first time, though he missed the boy and the sweet face of the mother, he was no longer under restraint. He could have her in his thoughts better than in his sight.

Many a year went by quietly, even happily, to James, for we find our highest happiness in doing our daily duties. He had earned his mother and sister a lovely home, which is much for any man single handed to do; was respected in the community, well read through his industry and perseverance, and a genial and good-principled citizen.

Nellie had married a widower with several motherless children, and she was doing for others what had been done for her. Then the good mother, when her time was fully come, died and was buried, and James was left alone.

Everybody supposed he would marry now; wondered why he was a bachelor! All the married ladies pitied him for their daughters' sakes, and ladies of uncertain ages looked wistfully in his direction. An old lady kept his house neatly, while in books and memories and social converse his days went by rapidly.

One morning the house went through an extra cleaning and arranging. An old schoolfriend, a bachelor like himself, was coming to spend several days with him, and the good housekeeper, a spinster herself, but old enough to be the mother of both of them, could not help feeling a little tremulousness with regard to the newcomer. James secretly felt more than ordinary interest in his coming, from the fact that Mrs. Stillson lived in the same place.

"I believe I have a friend in your vicinity," said James to his friend the first evening, at the supper table.

"Ah! I suppose some flame—a maiden lady about your age, probably."

"No. A Mrs. Stillson I refer to. We were very excellent friends when we were young."

"Indeed! I know her very well. Have done considerable law business for her since her husband's death. She has four children and in quite straitened circumstances."

James Matthews felt a sudden increase of circulation about his heart.

She was free to wed him now, if she would, he thought to himself. Now he could be a father to those children, and do for them all he had longed to do for her.

When the lawyer went home, much to his surprise Mr. Matthews accompanied him.

The knock at Mrs. Stillson's door was answered by a bright, noble-looking boy of eighteen. The mother, with the same sweet face as in her girlhood, was called in.

"Oh, James!" she said, and the tears gathered in her eyes. "I am so glad to see you once more!"

Perhaps she thought he held her hand too long and earnestly for a man who probably had a wife and children at home.

"I have thought," she added, "if I could only see you in our present circumstances, you might be induced to take our youngest, a boy of six, and adopt him as your own."

"Martha, may I take the boy, and take his mother with him?" said James Matthews, his heart almost too full for utterance.

The cheek was laid to his as in other days, and the old answer given, "Your will, James, is mine!"

He was satisfied now, with a happiness interwoven with it that none knew, except those who have waited long and been rewarded. The old housekeeper felt a little unpleasantly when a lady and four children were so suddenly added to their family, but soon recovered her equilibrium, and did everything for their comfort, living with them until she died.

There was considerable gossip for a time. Everybody knew now why he had not married earlier. The maiden ladies were quiet, the married ladies very polite, and James and Martha very happy in themselves and in their children.

WAIFY

"HEAVENS, a baby! Who brought such a speck of humanity to lay at my cold door? There is no love in my heart. The thing will die with me. I'll tuck it down in the corner of the cave for to-night."

Giles Mortimer laid the bundle on a rough pine table, put the candle close beside it, and one by one took off the garments folded about it—took them off with the same care and fear of touch as a naturalist in preparing the wings or feet of a fly for microscopic examination. He half raised it in his arms, then laid it down, walked around the cavern with a vague knowledge of a near presence, came back, took it up slowly and held it by the firelight.

It had a delicate girl-face, with half-quivering lips, and a little body perfect in proportions. Who was she? Some mother must have cared for her as long as strength or life lasted, for she was now fully ten months old. What should he do with the little waif? This triangular cave was his home. The green turf above it shut out scorching sun and chilling snow; the rude door before its opening made it seem secure from danger; the mortar he had put about the sides, the tall prairie grass he had matted over the ground floor, the old stove he had brought thither, the rustic chair he had made from the surrounding forests, and the Indian blankets he had bought for his bed, all made it comfortable, though gloomy.

Such a place might suffice for him, but how could an infant grow into grace and beauty here, leaning ever towards the light of the outer world, and longing for love that must be the elixir of life to woman?

The lips that before quivered with fear now opened with hunger. He laid her down, went out to a log box adjoining the cave, coaxed his goat to a fresh supply of milk, and the babe drank from his hand, nestled her head against his breast, and slept. She was not tucked away in a corner, but rested next his heart through that long night.

Giles Mortimer was written fatherless and motherless in boyhood. A pleasant home was sold, a small sum of money laid away, and a youth just needing a father's care and mother's affection was thrust upon the charities of the world. He soon found employment in a factory, and there, day by day, when others walked and laughed upon the highway, he worked and looked beyond to a successful future, saved his money carefully, dressed simply, and in a few years had nearly enough to defray the expenses of three years' study. College days followed. Those four years brought head and hand work to Mortimer. By forethought and exertion he gained the privilege of sweeping the college chapel, took the agency of books and pictures in vacation, and in numerous other ways partially paid for his education. His companions loved him for his geniality, and admired him for his broad grasp of mind and manly soul.

Life looked full of promise. Towards what should it tend? The professions were full. Among those who held out the gospel of life to the famishing, there were too many whom Christ had never called with His especial calling. There were lawyers at every corner quarrelling for a petty office, or looking over dusty books while sighing for the bright skies. There were teachers who needed to be taught. Chemistry, geology, and philosophy had so many votaries that only one in a century rose to eminence, and the remainder, in unsatisfying mediocrity, plodded on with little happiness to themselves and still less to others.

He turned to business. Here was an opening to gain honorable power by effort of will, by energy of hand, and by vigor of mind. There was beauty to him in the smoke that curled now lazily, now swiftly, from the chimneys of a hundred manufactories. If he could not be a merchant prince to give with blessed munificence one hundred thousand dollars for homes for the poor, he might have a home for some one who loved him, and many mites to scatter in the alleys of the great cities.

With Giles Mortimer's man-physique and mind there was a woman's sensitiveness, and a will that could not always bear the shock of opposition. A mountain is not all quartz, studded with jasper and amethyst, nor is it all trap, brown and coarse. All lives are elements from God's great storehouse, and earth a crucible which melts and moulds. He needed what most men need, the stimulus of love to give position or wealth or fame; the encouragement of a voice that has inspiration in it; the touch of a hand that carries hope in its pressure; the look of an eye that shines like a lone star on a dark night. He had seen some who might have walked beside him, but for his fear of taking them from a hall to a hovel.

He went to a strange city. Counting-rooms were filled, and clerkships engaged for months in advance. He knew no trade, or he might have worked and given honor to that. At last he obtained a place in a hardware establishment, and for two years, on a small salary, the student did uncongenial work to live; then the firm failed, and he was again adrift. He would have loved manufacturing; he would have been proud to have aided America with the labor of his brain and hands combined; but the old question, the one that has settled upon and crushed so many young men, came back—"What business can be carried on without money?"

Many men have struggled through poverty up to affluence. Many more have struggled in it down to a grave. There are not wanting those who tell us that every man may succeed, if he will; and yet ninety of every hundred who enter the whirlpool of trade are lost.

Like many others, when his heart was saddest he sang—sang like Carligny, who was dying when he made Paris intoxicated with his wit. No publisher was obtained for his poems; he had not found that spring that opens all portals—a name. Every house was already filled with manuscripts, every journal with hastily-written fragments. A living earned by writing was one that too often gave straw for a bed, and bread and water for food. He was growing tired of the battle. There were no victories—all defeats. Perhaps he lacked proper training of self; perhaps the now weakened physical had dimmed the mental; perhaps circumstances without were as strong as the powers within. Men were no longer brothers to him. He sighed for the freedom of solitude, stepped one evening on a freight train going West, and, careless for the future, went forward to an unknown fate. He crossed foaming Lake Erie; flat, woody Michigan and its lake; passed through Milwaukee with its forests and few inhabitants, where now rises one of the loveliest cities of the West, out into the uncivilized country. The land was rolling, with here and there a prairie shut in by a border of oak or cotton-wood trees. The lakes—long Pewaukee; graceful Pine; clear Kotchee, that makes the highway an arch and circles under it; and Neponset, with green, scalloped bank and a tree in each scallop reflected by the waters—all these were like oases to him.

He reached the Indian village, Oconomowoc, and stood at the foot of the peninsula that almost touches the island. On one side was a lake bordered with hawthorn, on whose bank a neat church now stands; on the other, five lakes, some small, one seventeen miles in length, surrounding islands covered with spruce and hemlock and oak. Hills, with their outcropping quarries of limestone, stood out against the blue sky. Back of this landscape, one of the most beautiful of the West, he found a cave worn into the mountain—a gloomy place, but free from dampness, and comfortable for one who had no care for humanity.

Occasionally he made friends with an Indian and asked him to his hut, but this was rare. They looked upon him as a pale-face who, having vexed the Great Spirit, was repenting in solitude. He spent his days in wandering and study. He learned the geological history of the place from the hieroglyphics God puts upon the rocks for man to read. He pressed hundreds of flowers, and knew what Jehovah had intended for the gardens of the growing West. He wrote some, and grew happy in his isolated existence; yet there was no flow of animal life within him, no leaping of the heart for joy. The past was a sealed book; the present written with the indifference of a stoic; and the future a blank leaf with no desire to write upon it.

Such was Giles Mortimer when a tender child was laid before him—a magnet to draw out a heart.

He called her Waify. For days and weeks he dressed her, washed her delicate clothes with his own hands, fed her, and made a wagon of rough boards and drew her to the lakes, that she might dabble her hands and feet in the clear waters. Soon the baby lips, as if taught by angels, said "Papa!" and the man's affections swept back upon him as a flood. He kissed her again and again, and she, all unconscious of the reason, put her fingers in his hair and beard, and laughed with that merry laugh that makes most homes, even in their decay, full of the echoes of childhood. A new look was born into his face, a look of manly protection, as though a soul was given to his charge.

Six months came and went. Little feet strolled outside the walls. She seemed to look vainly for something to play with, gathered blades of grass and flowers in her creeping, and showed a longing for a fuller life. Mortimer saw it, aroused his sleeping ambition, put out the fire in the old cave, put Waify into the wagon, with a blanket about her that he might keep in memory the first night she slept under it, tossed his half dozen books and small bundle of clothes at her feet, and started for the city. Kind people gave them a shelter at night, and Waify made friends everywhere.

To the home of a lady he had known among the early settlers of Milwaukee he carried his precious charge, and started this time for business with a strength and energy that knew no failure. There were some struggles, but at length a place was found with a land-broker. The city was growing rapidly. Small pieces of land were purchased as by economy some money was saved.

After many months of labor a small house was hired, a pretty play-room arranged for the wee Waify, a good servant obtained, and Giles Mortimer was a happy man. No longer hating the world or its

81

people, but having grown strong from obstacles overcome, he had sympathy for others and a genial look and manner that gave him the fascination of a woman.

Every night Waify came a little way to meet him. Then by the firelight he told her cheery stories, made rabbits for her on the wall, and with her on his knees thanked God for something human to love.

School life began. A tiny primer was purchased, and Mortimer, more the man than ever, taught her the alphabet. "A" she remembered from two rivers and a brook across. "B" was a river with two little crooked ones, and "C" stood for the cave. Every summer since they lived in the city he had taken her thither and showed her where she used to live.

"Here is the place where you were, Waify; here the table where I put my baby; here the old stove where I warmed your milk; here the green grass where you played."

"Pretty! pretty!" said Waify. "Kind papa to take care of me! Papa, when Waify dies will you bury her here among the flowers, and make a big 'C,' for cave, on the stone?"

A hurried kiss was the answer, while a shock that seemed like a premonition struck every nerve.

"Will you, papa? Will you?" pleaded the child. "Right here where the double daisies grow?"

"The garden will be gone, Waify."

"But won't you keep it for me, and bring me here?"

"Yes, darling. Yes, little one!" and they went home, the one light-hearted with the prospect of school again, the other saddened with a thought that seemed a prophecy.

A few days of joyous life went by. The little school-girl seemed less fond of play, more clinging to her adopted father, more thoughtful; then a slow fever, that seemed to have been inherited rather than the result of contagion, came on, and Waify, now scarcely out of her babyhood, was going to sleep through a long night.

Giles Mortimer watched her by day and by night, speechless; brought the toys she loved, and laid them beside her; brought the blocks of letters, and she took the "C" and put it under her pillow.

"Papa, we've had nice times together. Who'll be your little girl when Waify goes? Everybody has little girls. Perhaps somebody'll bring you one."

While he blessed God that she had been given to make him the man he was, he asked for no other in her place.

82

"But you must stay, Waify. I couldn't be happy without you."

"No, papa, I must go to ask God about my mamma, and perhaps I'll come back and tell you."

How little do children know of the land from whence there is no return!

The day looked for, dreaded, came.

"Where's the 'C,' papa?"

Clasping this tightly with one hand and Mortimer's with the other, looking sadly at the tears upon his cheeks, then joyfully out into the space, she said, "Kiss Waify!" and was dead.

Giles Mortimer's heart was mangled. The only thing he loved was taken.

There was a quiet gathering, and then he, with the sexton, took the little one to the cave, dug a grave under the daisies in the very centre of the garden, put a little tablet above it, and upon it the large marble "C" that stood for cave, and went back to his duties to work faithfully because her memory was something like her presence. The house was desolate, but sacred because Waify had been there. Business was interesting because entered upon for her; life was blessed because she had lived. Prosperity came to him. He loved other children, but there was only one Waify.

She had done her work. Through her love a man had known and found his manhood—had taken his true place in the world, in genial intercourse, in business power, in Christian benevolence. He has grown in position with the growth of a large city, but he still calls it home where a heart is buried, by the cave in Oconomowoc.

Perchance God told Waify of her mother, or told the mother of her child, for, weeks after her death, Giles Mortimer found upon the grave a touching token of a mother's love—a wreath of immortelles wrought into the word "Mother."

THE BLACK AND TAN

MRS. HENSON sat with her three children at their frugal supper. The house was neat, but very plain, and the dress of the children showed that they were only a trifle above actual want.

James, a boy of ten, sold newspapers and earned a little. Helen, between eight and nine, could help about the house when her mother was absent cleaning or washing, and Mary, seven, was the baby of the household, and the one for whom all the others sacrificed.

"Did you earn much this week, James?" said the mother, who had been a widow for several years. "You know I have been sick, and we can't meet the rent this month, and we didn't last month. I don't know what we shall do," said Mrs. Henson, in a tone of confidence with James, although she did not expect that her three small children could help her solve the problem. She knew that work alone would solve it, and this she was not always able to obtain, and had been too ill to labor even if the work were before her.

"I tried hard," said the brown-eyed, slender boy, "but I didn't sell as many papers as I do sometimes. I ran just as fast, but somehow I didn't get so many customers, and there weren't so many extras. You know a lady once in a while slips a nickel into your hand for a paper and won't wait for change, and that helps a fellow along. But I didn't have much of that last week. I didn't spend anything for myself, either."

"No, you wouldn't do that. We all save for each other since father died. We shall get over these hard places when you are a little older."

"Couldn't you borrow of the lady on the hill who gave me the shoes?" said Helen. "She seems very nice, and she is rich."

"She has been good to us," said the mother, "but I hate to bother her. One can wear out generous people by too constant asking for aid."

"I'll tell you what to do, mamma," said little Mary; "we'll sell the black and tan to the big gentleman who always speaks to me so kind."

"Oh, no!" said all the other voices together. "Blackie was given to you, and you have played with her, and we couldn't spare her. She eats very little, and you love her very much. She is the life of the house, she is so frolicsome."

"But he would pay money for her, and I could spare her if I had to. You said, mamma, we might be turned out of the house, and then what would Blackie do for a home? I think she would be happy in a big house, and we would give the man the basket she sleeps in, so she would be contented and remember us, too."

"Well, who would take her to the gentleman?" said Mrs. Henson. "I fear he would think it foolish."

"I will take her," said the child.

In the afternoon Mary wended her way to the mansion, with Blackie and the basket, and asked for the Hon. Mr. Colebrook. That gentleman rarely had time to see adults, but he would not refuse a child.

When he entered the room he found little Mary Henson with her basket and her dog, her eyes very red with weeping, and the dog whining as though she had heard the whole plan of separation from those she loved in the poor home.

"I've brought you my Blackie, sir, to sell her to you. Mamma needs money for rent, and as you are rich I thought you would like to buy her. She will love you very much, and kiss your face. She always sleeps with me, and perhaps she would sleep with you."

"And can you spare her?" said the millionaire. "I fear she would cry for her former home. It seems to me that you have been crying."

"Oh, yes, I did cry some when I kissed her the last time, and mamma and Helen and James all cried, because, you see, Mr. Colebrook, she is all we have to love!"

"Well, what do you ask for her?"

"I don't know. Mamma owes ten dollars for rent for the two months. I think, maybe, if you would pay that for her you could pay half now, and the landlady might wait for the other half, because she would know you would surely pay. I thought of selling Blackie to her, but Blackie needs a very nice home. Mme. Wainwright gave her to me, so you see Blackie comes from a good family, sir, and puts up with our poor home because we all love her so."

"Well, I will take her," said Mr. Colebrook, "and if she cries I will send for you to comfort her."

All this time Blackie was laying her head close to the child, as much as to say: "We will not be separated." When the millionaire attempted to take her she growled, and then looked plaintively toward her little mistress.

"He'll be very good to you, Blackie," said the child, who could not stop her tears. She wanted to sell the dog, and yet if she could only have the money and Blackie too! But that was impossible.

85

"I have no little girl to pet the dog," said the great man, "and I fear she will be lonely. You must come and see her," and he put the ten dollars into the child's hand, bade her good afternoon, and closed the door on a very sad little heart. Blackie crouched down in her basket as though the fine house were of no importance, and whined piteously for the little girl who had left her.

Mary sobbed all the way home, but she clasped the ten dollars tightly, and was thankful that they could all have a house over their heads for a little longer.

"I've brought the ten dollars, mamma," said the child, and she laid it in her mother's lap and stole away to weep alone over her sorrow.

Mrs. Henson was very sad over the matter. If she could earn but ten extra dollars! But she could not. The dog was probably not worth over a quarter of that sum, and the rich man had bought her just to help the family. Well, Blackie would have a home of luxury, and that was a comfort.

Hon. Mr. Colebrook had become interested in the child, and called at the little home a few days later to see how the widow and her family were prepared to meet the coming cold weather.

He asked for Mary. She was not well, the mother said, and had no appetite. "I suppose she misses Blackie," said Mrs. Henson, "though she never speaks of her."

"And the dog misses her, too, for she will neither eat nor play," said Mr. Colebrook. "I hope she will be better soon, for she is a winsome little creature. We are already fond of her."

"We are glad to have her in so good a home," said Mrs. Henson.

"How do matters look for the winter?" said the man of means. "Is the rent provided for, and the coal in the cellar?"

"I think we can get along now, since you kindly paid the rent for two months. I am in better health, and James seems to be selling more papers."

When Mr. Colebrook had gone Mary stole out to ask about Blackie. She could not go to see the dog,—that would give pain to two,—but she was eager to hear about her mute little playmate.

"Mr. Colebrook says Blackie will not eat much and misses you greatly," said Mrs. Henson. A smile crept over the child's face as she said: "I thought Blackie really loved me. I would go to see her if she wouldn't feel bad when I came away, and I mustn't make her heart ache."

"Oh, I think she'll forget about us all soon, and enjoy her new home very much!" said Helen.

86

"I think not," said Mary. "Blackie never forgets. She never did."

It was late in the autumn, and Mrs. Henson was too busy with work to think much more about a dog. James was up early and home late, and Helen's little hands were more than filled with work too hard for a child.

Christmas was near at hand, and the rich and the poor were planning according to their means for a merry time. Mrs. Henson's presents must necessarily be small, and along the line of the absolutely necessary. James must have boots, Helen a simple dress, and Mary some mittens, with a bag of parched corn, a little candy, and a few nuts.

Mr. Colebrook did not forget the widow's family. He sent coal, a barrel of flour, some money for rent, and some articles of clothing for the children. There was one quite large package for Mary. What was in it nobody could imagine, though Mrs. Henson was in the secret. Finally a low whining was heard; the box was hastily opened, and out sprang Blackie into Mary's lap, and kissed her over and over again. The child cried, and Blackie nestled her face against Mary's neck and cried also. She was home again as a Christmas present, and she liked the plain home better than the grand one.

"Did you really want to come back, Blackie," said Mary, "and sleep with me again, and not be rich and great any more?" and Blackie wagged her tail and whined approvingly, as though it were the happiest Christmas of her life.

"THIS IS Mr. Graham, a leader in our church work," said Miss Ward, as she introduced the fine-looking young man to her friend Miss Warburton.

"Oh, yes!" said the person addressed. "I remember seeing you at the lakes last summer. What a pleasant company we had at the hotel!"

"Yes, but I went especially for the shooting. Such fine game up there! Birds of many kinds, ducks, and now and then a deer. I went just for sport, though I didn't care much about the things after they were shot. We went fishing one day, and the fish were so small we let a quantity die in the bottom of the boat rather than carry them home. We had quite an excitement one day when we found we had killed a robin and her youngsters were in a nest close by with open mouths."

"What did you do with the little birds?" said Miss Warburton.

"Oh, they had to starve, of course!"

"And did you bring home the mother bird?"

"No, she was pretty badly hurt, and couldn't live long. We had so many ducks and other things that we couldn't carry all of them."

"Don't you feel badly to leave a wounded robin or duck to die slowly?"

"Oh, we men haven't women's hearts, Miss Warburton, or we shouldn't shoot at all, I fear!"

"I never could see how a Christian man could find pleasure in giving pain. I know some of our professing Christians have hunted buffaloes on the American plains, and left them to die, just for the sport of killing, as some of the English hunters do in South Africa. And I suppose some who hunt foxes, and find pleasure in seeing dogs catch and tear them to pieces, profess Christianity."

"Well, you ladies are eager to ride fast and get the brush."

"I should not be. I would not take the tail of the fox after the poor thing had been frightened nearly to death before capture. We think bull-fights in Spain, where animals are killed for sport, brutal and wicked; but we seem to think that where foxes are killed for sport it is only a pleasant and exhilarating pastime. Does the size of the animal make the difference?"

"I think, Miss Warburton, you would deprive us of all pleasure. Nothing is more bracing than the eager run with the dogs over fields and fences, and the rivalry in reaching the game first is very exciting."

"And the next day or the next week you come back and lead a prayer meeting, and urge us to be gentle and tender, and trust in Him who lets not even a sparrow fall to the ground without his notice! I think Cowper was right when he said—

"'I would not enter on my list of friends
(Though graced with polished manners and fine sense,
Yet wanting sensibility), the man
Who needlessly sets foot upon a worm.'"

"But, Miss Warburton, you must remember that animals are killed for food for you and me, and for others."

"That should be done as humanely as possible, Mr. Graham. Our stock-yards and places for killing animals should all be under the most careful city or State supervision. We can easily brutalize people. At first, most men and women shrink from inflicting pain or shedding blood, but even those high in church or State can become callous to cruelty."

"I fear you wouldn't approve of letting ministers and presidents have a little fun from shooting."

"No, not if that 'fun' took even birds away from their young, and helpless creatures were shot for the mere pleasure of shooting. The Princess of Wales, thanks to her womanly heart, has helped to put an end to pigeon-shooting for sport, and balls are found to answer the purpose."

"This is getting personal. I fear you will not enjoy having me lead our meetings and asking sinners to become converted."

"You are quite right, Mr. Graham. Some persons may not feel as I do, but for myself it greatly lessens the force of your words or prayers. I have spoken plainly because I believe your killing for sport has a bad influence over others. To me it does not seem consistent with your profession of kindness and love to all of God's creatures. I hope you are not offended."

"Oh, no, far from it! You have set me thinking. It has been thoughtlessness on my part, for as a leader in Christian things I want to do what is right."

"I THINK George Thomas is fond of Edith, for he comes to the house often, and always gives her a delicate deference which shows his appreciation of woman."

"Yes," said Mr. Sinclair in reply to his wife, "Thomas is a good fellow, a hard worker, economical, and worthy of any girl, though of course he isn't rich. That doesn't matter, however, for I have enough for Edith. I've often wondered why he didn't offer himself."

"I can't imagine," replied his wife, "except that he does not earn enough to support Edith in the way she has been accustomed to live. Young men are unduly sensitive about that, when often the young woman would value a true affection more than a fine house and surroundings. I am sure Edith is fond of him, for although she says nothing her face and manner show it."

"I don't see how we can help matters, wife. Probably time will settle it."

But time did not settle it, for Edith Sinclair, for some unexplained reason, was growing pale and listless. Something was wearing her nerves, and at last she was really ill. Naturally frail, and loving one to whom she could not make known her feelings, the repression, uncertainty, and perhaps surprise that no word was spoken finally culminated in her illness.

A physician was called, a woman who had long been the friend of the family; she divined some trouble that was not apparent to the world. One morning when she came, taking Edith's hand she said, "Dear, I think something is worrying you. Would you mind telling me so that I can help you, perhaps?"

"There is nothing to be done, doctor," said the girl sadly, as tears came into her large, dark eyes. "I have everything in this beautiful home, but I don't care for it."

"But what would make you happy—to go away for a time and have change of air and scenery?"

"No, I would rather stay here. I am too tired to go away."

"Edith, I must tell you what I think is the truth. You love Mr. Thomas, and are unwilling that he or anybody should know it."

"I admire him very much," said the girl slowly.

"But why have you never let him see that you liked him?"

"I couldn't do that, doctor. He knows that we are good friends."

"Has he ever spoken of marriage?"

"No."

"Would you marry him if he asked you?"

"If he loved me—never without."

"What if I should find out his feelings for you?"

"Oh, not for the world, doctor! Let that come of his own free will if at all."

"But you are ill, child, and you are letting the matter prey upon your strength and health. Mr. Thomas is a noble young man, and I believe is fond of you."

"We must wait, doctor. I shall be better soon."

Mr. Thomas called a few days later, but Edith was too ill to see him, and he left his regrets with her parents. He went home sadly to think of his future. He loved Edith, he was happy in her refined society, but his salary was not large, and he could not support her as he desired. She would tire of the home he could give her, and be unhappy, he thought. He called again, but as before was unable to see Edith.

He finally resolved to talk with her parents and tell them of his love for her, and why he had waited until he was better able to provide for her; but she was an only child, and he hesitated to commit himself. Others liked her, and he loved her too well to take her into privation. Besides, the parents, while they liked him, might not be at all willing to give him their daughter. He would talk with her physician, and she, a woman, would know whether Edith were really interested in him.

He called upon Dr. Mary Armstrong as soon as possible.

"I have come to ask about my friend, Miss Sinclair," he said, as he sat in the physician's parlor. "Is she better?"

"No, she does not mend at all. There seems to be some weight upon her heart or life that is breaking her down."

The blood came to the young man's face, but how could he know that "the weight" upon her heart meant love for him! Perhaps he was too presuming. After an awkward silence he said, "Doctor, I must confide in you. I love Miss Sinclair, but I have never had the means to marry her. I have had a mother and sister to make a home for, and I could not ask another to share my poverty. I do not know that Edith returns my affection, though we have had a delightful friendship together."

"She loves you, I feel sure," said her doctor, "and I think your mistake has been that you and she have not had an understanding sooner. Edith is a sensitive, lovely girl, delicately reared, and almost too careful of the conventionalities of life, or she would have shown her love for you."

"Do you think the time has come to tell her that I love her?"

"Perhaps not just yet. I will tell her of our conversation and make her ready for the meeting."

Young Thomas went away with a lighter heart than he had had for months. At last Edith would know all and wait for him, if she loved him.

Dr. Armstrong came every day to the Sinclair home, but the sick girl grew no better. Soon after this talk with Mr. Thomas the doctor said to Edith, "I have had a visit from your friend, and, just as I expected, he loves you, but has never asked your hand in marriage because he has so many cares at home and a small salary."

The white face grew eager and flushed with color. "I told him," Dr. Armstrong continued, "that he had made a mistake in not having an understanding with you, and then both could wait for marriage if circumstances made such waiting wise. Do you want to see him, Edith?"

"Yes, as soon as I am a little stronger. I feel too weak to-day."

Several days passed, and strength did not return rapidly, but a new peace had come into Edith's life, for she loved and was beloved, and then there was a happy meeting of the two lovers, but a quiet one of few words and promises.

Weeks and months went by, during which time hope and love worked the same miracle that has been wrought thousands of times since the world began.

Edith walked in the sunshine of a new day and a new life of restored health and vigor. The autumn leaves took on their color, and red showed itself again in the young girl's cheeks.

When Christmas day came, that precious day of giving and receiving, George Thomas and Edith Sinclair gave themselves to each other for life.

AN UNFORTUNATE SAIL

"THE SUNSET is so lovely we might take a row on the ocean," said Mr. Farneaux to the young lady who was walking beside him.

"I don't quite like to go on Sunday evening," said the girl. "But we wouldn't stay long, would we?"

"Oh, no, only till the sun went down! And we have just come from church, so where's the harm?"

So a little rowboat was engaged for an hour, and two happy persons pushed off the Jersey Island coast. They chatted merrily as the red and yellow of the clouds played on the waters, and let the boat half drift toward the sunset.

Suddenly the young man dropped one of the oars. A shade of fear passed over Louise Arnot's face.

"Can you reach it?" she asked anxiously.

"Oh, yes, don't fear!" and he took the other oar and guided the boat toward the missing paddle.

The breeze was blowing off the land, and increasing. The boat was not easily managed with one oar, and the cheery face of young Farneaux grew a little troubled as the oar drifted faster than the boat.

Anxiety does not give a steady hand, and before he knew it the other oar had slipped from his grasp.

Miss Arnot's face grew white. "What shall we do? We are drifting out to sea. Would they see us if we were to signal to the shore? Ours is the only boat out. Oh! why did we start at all?"

"Accidents will happen. I must jump for the oars. I am a good swimmer. Don't get frightened and let the boat tip and fill with water. I'll soon be back."

"But you may be drowned," said the frightened girl. "I wish I could swim, and so help you."

"No, no! Keep the boat steady as I jump, and I'll have them in hand soon. I must throw off this coat, so I can swim." He rose, put his hand on the side, and gave a leap into the ocean.

Her heart sank within her as he went, but there was nothing else possible to be done.

The boat, lightened of its freight, glided on further and further from shore. She wished she were heavier to hold it down. She wished she could reach one oar while he obtained the other, as both had now floated far apart. She watched him breathlessly as he swam

93

away. Impeded somewhat by his clothes, he yet swam hastily and caught one oar, holding it up to Louise's delighted eyes.

He did not see that the boat was drifting fast away from him. But he must have the other oar. Both persons were helpless without it, so he redoubled his efforts. He felt the breeze stiffening. What if he could not reach the oar? What if he could not reach the boat with its fair owner? What if Louise were to drift out to sea and be drowned, and her death be laid at his door? No, that should not be; and he put his whole strength against the waves. He gained in speed, and soon held the coveted oar in his grasp.

He looked toward the skiff. Alas! it was smaller to his sight and almost flying before the wind. He started with the oars, but he felt himself weakening. He must throw them away if he would overtake the boat, and then it would be certain death to both. The moments were agonizing. Even if he did reach Louise, he could not swim with her to the shore. If he reached the bank himself, he could get friends to put out and save her.

Thus reasoning, he sorrowfully dropped the oars and swam for life. The wind had now become violent and he was losing strength, but fear and despair nerve us to our uttermost; and finally, well nigh exhausted, he touched the shore. He was grateful, but almost overcome with sorrow as well as fatigue.

An excited crowd gathered around him.

"Where is the young lady?" they asked.

"We lost the oars, and she has drifted out to sea. God help her!"

"Coward!" shouted the crowd, who are usually blind and unreasoning.

"Nobody'll believe such a yarn," said one.

"We heard cries of 'Murder!' 'way back here on the shore," shouted others, for there is always a class of persons who fill life with imaginary evils, as though it were not full enough of real ones.

"Arrest him—he deserves lynching," said others, who knew and honored the young girl who was now missing.

"Man a boat and let us go and bring her back," persisted young Farneaux, but the people laughed him to scorn. The case was plainly against him. He had taken her out and came back without her. He could swim and she could not, and he had basely deserted or murdered her. Besides, no rowboat could live in the fast-increasing waves. The officers hurried Farneaux off to jail, and he was indicted for homicide. In vain he protested; in vain he begged for clemency till the matter could be investigated. No, they would keep him close in hand, and if anything favorable developed they would give him the benefit.

Meantime what had become of the rowboat? It had drifted out into the deep ocean with its helpless occupant. The sun went down in a blaze of light, but the beautiful red and orange colors brought no joy to the eyes that peered in vain toward the horizon.

"Mr. Farneaux would not desert me," she murmured. "Where can he be?" and she shaded her eyes with her hand, hoping to see the dim outline of a human being.

The stars came out slowly one by one, and gradually she knew that she was at the mercy of the great ocean and the God who rules over all. What might come she hardly dared to think. If a storm did not arise, she might float on and on. If the wind rose higher, more water would come into the boat, for it dipped already, and then death was certain.

She began to grow hungry and faint, but she must not give up. The hours grew toward midnight. There was no use to call aloud, for there was no soul to respond. The boat lurched, and was now half full of water. She could only pray and wait in agony.

One hour, two hours, three hours, four hours, five hours, which were as long as weeks, and then the sun streaked the eastern sky, and came up as grandly and joyously as though no hearts were breaking on land or sea.

"O Father in heaven, if some ship might only pass this way!" she moaned. So thirsty, but no water—so hungry, but no food—weak from loss of sleep, but with nerves strung to their utmost tension in the eager watching for a sail.

The whole forenoon passed. The mid-day sun grew hot and parching, and hope was finally giving way to despair. The whole of life had been reviewed, with thoughts of the dear ones waiting for her. The whole afternoon dragged on, the sun set, and the second weary night was to be lived through, or death might come before morning. Hunger and fear had blanched the face, and death even was beginning to lose its terrors from the numbness of the physical.

The night wore away, long and weary and desolate, and again morning dawned. Louise was sitting in the water of the boat, her limbs chilling, scarce knowing now if she were dead or alive. It was growing toward noon again; forty hours alone on the ocean, and death seemingly near at hand.

Something appeared in the distance. What! Did she see with her half-blind eyes the smoke of a coming vessel? Could it be, or was it only a mirage which had deceived again and again?

Yes, it actually came nearer; but would it see her, a mere speck on the ocean? She would gather strength enough to wave her handkerchief. Ah! it really was a vessel. God help her now in her one last gleam of hope! She had no strength to call, and even if she had probably such call would be useless. How earnestly she prayed, gaining new lease of life from this new hope!

"There's something ahead," said the man at the lookout. "Perhaps a body floating out at sea; no, it looks like a rowboat—perhaps a drifting lifeboat of some steamer." And word was given to bring the ship alongside.

"Heaven help us—why, there's a girl in the boat alone!"

"Lower a lifeboat, boys, and pull out for her."

"Aye, aye, sir!" said the men, with eager hearts, for none have warmer than those who sail the ocean.

Louise's heart bounded for joy when she saw the sturdy oarsmen come near. She would have fainted hours before, but now she wept with gratitude.

"It's a long way ye are from home," said one broad-shouldered sailor, as he lifted her in his arms like a child, and carried her into the lifeboat.

She was too weak to tell the story now, and wondering how it all happened the men carried back their precious freight to the ship.

The captain and officers showed her every kindness, offering her food when she could partake of it, and giving her every chance for rest and sleep.

"But we cannot take you home," said the kind-hearted man. "We are on our way to America. It must be weeks before our return."

"I am so thankful for all your kindness. I can wait anywhere, only so I send them word of my safety."

The steamer arrived on the Atlantic coast May 19, just one month after the almost fatal boat-ride.

On the other side of the ocean there was sorrow and suspense. Louise's home was desolate for its lost one. Public opinion was still bitter against the author of her misfortune. With innocent heart, but blanched face, Mr. Farneaux was brought from jail to the crowded court-room for his trial on the charge of homicide. Every day and hour he had hoped for some word that would show him to be guiltless, but days grew into weeks, and neither the boat nor Louise Arnot was found. He supposed her dead, but hoped some vessel would report the empty boat, or have picked up at sea the missing one.

The prosecution made out a strong case.

"If Mr. Farneaux's story were true," said the attorney, "that he was unable to reach her, and therefore saved his life by swimming ashore, her body would have been found on the beach long before this. She was last seen in his company. It was an easy matter to sink the oars and then swim to shore after the deed was done. Thirty days have gone by, long enough for any vessel to have picked her up and restored her to her heart-broken family, if she were alive."

And then for hours the enormity of the deed, the coaxing her to go upon the ocean that Sabbath evening, the cold-bloodedness of the whole affair, were gone over by able lawyers.

Mr. Farneaux's face grew white, and his body trembled at the accusations. And then he told in straightforward language the story of his losing the oars, of the increasing wind so that he could scarcely gain the shore, of the impossibility of reaching her with his heavy oars in hands, and of the certainty of death for both if he attempted it.

"He talks like an innocent fellow," said one.

"Yes, I have known him for years, and he's a well-brought-up young man, but I've known well-brought-up people turn out to be fiends," said another.

"Not often if they have Christian parents," said a third. "That young man has a good mother, and it's rare that the son of such a mother goes wrong. I believe in the man. I'd be willing to wager a good deal that his story is true."

Several witnesses testified as to good character, but one fact was patent to all, that Louise Arnot went out with him and he came back alone, excited, anxious, and seemingly greatly disturbed. He could prove nothing, and circumstances were against him.

Away in America the sick girl, now coming to her usual health by care, was writing a cable message the hour the ship arrived. "How glad they will be! Poor Mr. Farneaux will be so anxious. He swam for the boat, I know, just as long as he could."

So the words were sent: "Louise Arnot picked up at sea in open boat. Arrived in New York May 19. Well."

A courier came to the crowded court-room and delivered the message. A hush fell upon the assembly, and then a cheer broke out, and tears rolled down the cheeks of the man accused of murder. The proceedings were stayed, and the townspeople waited eagerly for the coming of Miss Arnot, that she might tell the story of why she was left alone through those terrible forty hours.

The captain had taken Miss Arnot to his home till she should fully recover and be able to make the return voyage. One day as she was reading the daily paper her eye fell upon the words, "Supposed murder at sea," and where was detailed the arrest of Mr. Farneaux and his unexpected deliverance by her cable.

"What if I had not been rescued," she said, "and had died in the boat! Who could have saved my poor, dear friend then?" And anew she thanked God for her miraculous deliverance, and for saving the life of her friend.

A few weeks later Miss Arnot was home in her beloved island, her friends gathering about her. All were eager for her side of the story. "Mr. Farneaux has told the truth," she said, "and I am more thankful for his life even than for my own. What would have been my agony if he had suffered death for me!"

Time will tell what the sequel will be! Whatever life has before them, neither will forget the awful experience of being on the sea alone, drifting helplessly, or on trial for murder with no power to prove one's innocence. And each is thankful for that wonderful deliverance.

A NEW KIND OF WEDDING

"I DO NOT want the usual kind of wedding," said the pretty daughter of Jared Strong, the millionaire of Huntsville. "I would rather use the money spent for flowers and supper in a way that pleases me better."

"And what would please you?" said the gracious man, who loved his daughter with an especial fondness now that her mother was dead. "You are a queer girl."

"I will spend the money wisely, if I may have it."

"But what will the young man you are to marry think of a simple and private wedding, and what will the people in society think, who have entertained you?"

"They know already that I care little for parties or clubs. Going into one of the 'Settlements' and seeing how the poor live cured me of extravagance. Why, the money spent for one grand party would make one hundred poor people comfortable for a year!"

"Well, the suppers and making the fine silks give employment to people," said Mr. Strong.

"But you forget, father, how much further the money would go if spent otherwise. A florist receives one thousand dollars for flowers. His family and a few workmen are benefited, but that thousand dollars would keep scores of families from starving or cold, if properly used. Many, unable to obtain work,—and we know from statistics that quite a large per cent. cannot possibly get it, because there is not work enough for all,—would be cheered and kept from discouragement if rent could be paid for a time, or clothes furnished, or coal given, or comforts provided in sickness."

"Do as you wish, my child. You shall have the money to spend as you like. I fear, however, that the world will call you peculiar. You know there has always been poverty and always will be."

"But we who are rich have duties to those who are not so fortunate. I learned at the 'Settlement' how the luxuries of the rich make the poor feel discouraged and unhappy. They work, and they see idlers all about them who are haughty when they should be kind and courteous. The poor see many of the rich waste their time in hunting or useless pleasure. They see people living for self, with no thought of the homeless or over-worked. They see clothes thrown away or hoarded, when they might be of use to somebody."

"What does my dear Louise wish for her wedding day? No jewels and laces and rejoicing over the happy event?"

"Well, let us see how much I can save to use as I like. I prefer to be married quietly in our own home, with only a few friends together. I do not want many outside presents, for people give more than they can afford generally, and because they feel that social customs demand it. The flowers, if the church and house were elaborately trimmed, would cost a thousand dollars, the supper for a large company another thousand, the elegant wardrobe, which I do not wish, another thousand. Now I would rather have this to spend for myself."

"You shall have it, daughter, and we will see how you will spend it. You will be the talk of Huntsville."

Louise Strong, college educated, was about to marry a young man who was graduated from the same class as herself. He had wealth and did not need her fortune; besides, he loved her well enough to let her decide what would make her happiest.

Soon after leaving college she entered one of the college "Settlements," partly because some of her friends were trying the experiment, and partly because she had an interest in those less fortunate than herself. She found it true, indeed, that "one-half the world does not know how the other half lives."

While one part dressed in purple and fine linen and fared sumptuously every day, another had scarcely enough to eat or to wear, slept on poor beds if any, with insufficient bedding to keep them from the cold, in tumble-down tenement houses, with high rents and no conveniences. With pinched faces and oftentimes bitter hearts they looked on the showy equipages, elegant mansions, and extravagant dresses of many of the rich.

True, there were some who, either because of their refined tastes or Christian principles, made little display, and gave of their surplus to bless humanity, but the majority lived for self and let the rest of the world struggle as it might. They would not take on responsibility, and in no wise regarded themselves as holding their property in trust for the betterment of the world. They had made their money and they would spend it as they chose. To God or man they did not feel responsible. Only when death came did they begin to ask if life had been well spent.

Louise Strong had gone into poor homes and cared for sick children; she had given sympathy and money; she had read to weary and lonely persons; she had encouraged the despondent, tried to find situations for those out of work, helped to make the "Settlement" a social home and place of elevation and rest, and learned, best of all, that life is worse than useless unless lived for the sake of others.

And now what should she do with the three thousand dollars

100

that were to be spent for the wedding if she did not use them in charity? There were so many ways to spend it that one could scarcely select. The libraries needed more books; some of the children in the Sunday School of her church needed proper clothing; the people in jails ought to have books and papers; the poor who hesitated to ask charity because it was so often grudgingly given at the public institutions, and often to the unworthy, needed coal and food and clothes; many boys and girls longed for a college education and were helpless in getting it; the colored people in the South needed education and to be taught industries; the temperance cause needed money and workers. How should she use her three thousand dollars?

One of the friends she had made at the "Settlement," Alice Jameson, had often said she wished she could visit among the poor and be their friend, but she had no means. Louise knew that personal contact with human beings is the best way to improve them. She went to see her friend Alice.

"I have a proposition to make," she said to Alice. "I can have the money for my wedding to use as I please. How would you like to be my missionary? I to pay you a salary, and you to visit in your own field and tell me all the needy and helpless, so that you and I can find a way to brighten their lives."

"I should be more delighted than you can imagine," said Alice. "Call me the 'Louise Missionary.' And now, as the cold weather is coming, I think you will want to provide me with one or two hundred pairs of mittens and warm stockings, and perhaps you will like to use some of the money in Christmas gifts for those who rarely have presents."

"Capital," said Louise. "And I have another suggestion. I love animals so much, dogs and horses especially, that I want children taught to be kind to them. Let us put two hundred copies of 'Our Dumb Animals,' each fifty cents a year, into as many homes, for nobody can read that paper without being kinder all his life."

Louise Strong was married quietly to one of the noblest men of the city, and Alice Jameson began her labor of love. After one year of work, and gifts supplied by Louise, of course a generous father and husband would not see the enterprise abandoned. The incidents of the next few years, told by Alice to Louise, the dying cared for, children saved and placed in good homes, men helped and women cheered, would fill a volume. Louise, thus kept in touch with the world's sorrow, did not forget and become selfish. How many lives were blessed with that wedding money!

LOST HIS PLACE

"WE ARE sorry to let you go, James, but business is dull and we must cut down expenses."

The speaker was the head of a hardware store, a man not unkind in nature, but who looked at business purely as a money-making matter. Men were not to be carried over a long winter if there was no need for their help.

James Leonard's eyes fell on the paper where he was writing with a sadder expression than before, but he said nothing. Both of his parents were dead. He was not strong in body, and none too well fitted to cope with the obstacles one meets in the daily struggle for existence. He would, of course, look for work, but that it was not easy to find he had proved when attempting to get a situation several months before. He had very little money saved for his board, for wages had been small. He would keep his inexpensive room, eat but two meals a day, if need be, and hoped his money would last till a place could be found.

The next morning he started out, not over-courageous, but determined to be persevering. From store to store, from office to office, he asked for work, and received the same old reply—"We are discharging men, rather than hiring new ones." Days went by and grew into weeks. He came home hungry, cold, and tired. There was nobody to confer with or to cheer him. He could not get bookkeeping—that was hopeless. He would take any kind of work that could be obtained, for his money was growing perilously scant.

Finally, despite his delicate appearance, a man hired him at small wages at heavy outdoor work. As might have been expected, his hands were soon blistered, insufficient food left him with little strength, and he broke down from the labor.

The woman at whose house James had his room cared for him as best she could, but she also was poor and could not long provide for him without remuneration. He must have money for food and fuel. He could not go to the poorhouse, he could not go to a hospital while half-way able to work, and he had no relatives upon whom he could depend.

Resolutions to do right are sometimes broken when everything seems against a person. James was cold and needed an overcoat. Possibly he could have begged one; possibly not, for the world is not over-generous with overcoats. He saw one in the hall of a house which he was passing; the night was bitter cold—he opened the unfastened door, stole the coat, and hurried away.

He was restless that night as he attempted to sleep. He was cold, and in his dreams put on an overcoat that did not fit him, and he felt ill at ease. As he wore it next day, though it was black, he thought everybody looked at it. The owner might recognize it by the cut of the collar or the sleeves. He was not happy, but he was warm, and by and by, as he walked, he forgot that the coat was not really his own and paid for with his own money.

He could find nothing to do in the city. He could go out into the suburbs; perhaps in the homes of wealth they would feel neither the hard times nor the need for retrenchment in winter. He walked all day, and slept in a barn at night. The next day he went from house to house, and there was no more success than before.

As night came on he passed a beautiful home back from the street, where the windows were lighted and all seemed inviting and happy. He looked in at the window. The daughter of the house sat reading in the cosey library, and a servant was preparing supper in the kitchen.

He walked away, and then went back. There must be a good deal of food in so cheerful a home, and he needed some. He had asked for food before this, and sometimes a kind lady gave him hot coffee with his bread and butter, but oftener the servants refused.

He would wait till later, and then, unperceived, he would enter the pantry and take what he needed for the night and the day following. It was cold remaining outside, and the hours to wait seemed very long, but then he was used to waiting for everything. There was little else for him to do nowadays.

The lights were turned out early, for there had been a party at the house the previous night. He lifted the slightly fastened kitchen window, entered the pantry, and ate what food he needed, filling his pockets for the next day's use.

He was going away when something bright gleamed before him. It was a basket of silver ready to be put into the safe, but carelessly left for the morrow. That, if sold, would give him money enough to last the winter through.

He had to think and act quickly. Before he had time to argue with himself the right or the wrong of it he had gathered all and put it into a satchel close at hand. The satchel was heavy, but he hurried away, secreting some of it, after he left the house, near or partly under a stone wall.

He feared somebody on the street would hear the silver rattle, or somebody in the street-car would hit his foot against it. Every eye seemed upon the satchel, and he was glad to get out of the car and take it to a pawn-shop. As usual, the pawn-broker beat him down in the price of the silver. He knew the young man's necessities and offered him not over a fifth of its value. Young Leonard demurred, but finally took the money and hurried away.

Again he looked for work and found some for a day or two. He used his money carefully, and when it was gone went stealthily to the hidden place by the wall, dug up the silver, and took it to the pawn-broker. The police had an agreement with the dealer in stolen goods, and when Leonard came again to sell he was arrested, tried, and sentenced to prison.

The prison years, as those know who have tried them, went by painfully, with much of depression, much of good resolutions, much of hopelessness, much of weariness and mortification. When James Leonard was released he determined to begin life anew. He had the same old struggle to obtain a place, but finally succeeded as the coachman for two ladies. He was faithful, honest, and greatly liked by them.

One day a policeman recognized him. "Hello, James," he said, "glad to see you in a good home. How did they happen to take you? Did they know you had been in prison?"

"Oh, no, and I wouldn't have them for the world! They wouldn't trust me, and would turn me off."

"But they'll find it out, I fear. Better be straight, I think. I would tell all and take my chances. If they hear it from outside you'll be sure to lose your place."

The next persons to recognize James were two servants, who, eager to be the bearer of news, told the cook who worked in the same house with James. To her a prison seemed an awful thing, and she told the ladies. They in turn told James they feared to trust a man who had stolen, and discharged him. They did not stop to ask themselves where the man would go for a home if they turned him away.

The old result happened. James searched for a situation, did not succeed, became discouraged, was without funds, stole, and again was sent to prison.

It is easy to say that James Leonard should have been strong enough to resist temptation. It is easy to say that all men and women can find places if they try long enough. At the same time, there is a responsibility resting upon the employer of labor when of necessity a man loses his position. To be our brother's keeper is a vital point in a Christian community.

STRUCK IT RICH

"IT'S NO USE, Martha," said Asa Scranton to his wife, as he came in from the street, tired and discouraged. "I've tried day after day for a job, and I've come to the conclusion that you and the children are better off without me than with me."

"Oh, no, Asa!" responded the pale, thin woman, who was cooking dinner for some workingmen who boarded with her. "We shall see better days."

But her words only were hopeful; the voice showed the weariness of one who was almost tired of the daily struggle.

"I don't know how it is. I've worked hard from a boy. The grocery business didn't pay, though I never left the store till the last man had gone home. Then the builder I worked for failed, and I lost several months' wages. I guess I'm unlucky. We had quite a bit of money when we married, didn't we, Martha? And I never supposed you would come to such hard work as this. My debts have hung like a millstone about my neck. They all say: 'Asa Scranton, you're a good fellow. You'll pay principal and interest,' and never think that a wife and children have need for food and clothing. Sometimes I've a mind to run away, and I would if I didn't hate a coward. I can't stand seeing you so pale and hopeless-like. I'd like to try the mines—maybe I'd strike it rich."

"Oh, Asa, don't think of such a thing! Only the few make any money in mines, and most are poor to the end of their days. Keep up courage. The children are getting larger, and better days are coming."

"That's the old story, Martha. Things are not very even in this world, but I don't complain. If I had work I wouldn't care how rich other folks are. But just think, Martha! If I strike a mine, as some people have, how good it would seem for you to have a silk dress, and Alice a hat with a feather, like the little girl on the hill. I always wanted John to go to college, seeing that his father couldn't go. He maybe would be more lucky than I have been."

While Martha Scranton mended by the open fireplace that evening, Asa sat still and thought—dreamed dreams, half wildly perhaps, of better days to come. They would never come in his present poverty. He would make one last venture. His family could live without him, for his wife for some time had earned all the money which they used.

He was not an indolent man, not a man who lacked ability, but, like thousands of others, he seemed to be in the current of failure, and was drifting down the stream to despair. He dreamed about the mines of Colorado that night as he slept, and during the many waking hours planned how he could reach the favored land. He could sell his silver watch, and pawn his overcoat, even if the coming winter pinched him with cold.

By morning he had decided. He ate breakfast quietly; patted little John upon the head, with a look of unusual pathos in his blue eyes; told Martha that he was going out to look for work; obtained what little money he could; hurried down the street to the station, wiping, with the back of his hand, the tears from his cheeks as he looked only once toward his home; and took the train for the mines.

For days he ate little, hoarding every cent to keep him from starvation till he should find work. At Granite Camp, on the side of the mountain, all was bustle and confusion. The varied machinery, the eager miners, the enthusiasm, the warm-hearted familiarity,— all excited Asa. He was ready for any kind of work, and soon found it. Mining was hard,—no work is easy,—but he would earn and save, and later prospect for himself, get hold of claims, and "strike it rich."

Weeks and months passed. No letter came from Martha, for she did not know where Asa had gone. She wept when she found that she was left alone—wept with that half-deadened sense of loss which persons feel who have had the cheer of life taken out of them by the blows of circumstance.

Asa had been kind to her and the children, but in these days she had little time to think of love or loss, for work was never-ending, and rent and fuel were certainties. So she toiled on, and guessed that he had gone to seek his fortune in the mines, and clothed the children as well as she could, and sewed and washed and prayed and waited.

Years came and went. Asa Scranton in the mines and Martha Scranton at home were growing older. The miners liked Asa, though he joined little in their merry-making, and got the name of being miserly. They could not know that he was saving his money to make Martha rich. Sometimes, when he had earned money enough to work a claim, and had gotten other parties interested, he dug for treasure, but always failed. Then the hole was left in the mountain, and Asa went back to his daily digging in the mines.

His hair grew grayer and his form bent. He would write Martha and Alice and John when he had made his fortune, but not now. He lived alone in his little shanty, often weary, always lonely, "forever unlucky," as he said, but still hoping that better days would come. Every spare moment he searched the mountains, till it was common talk that Asa Scranton knew every vein of silver and lead in the surrounding country. He would make one last effort. He had been to one spot stealthily, from time to time, where, from the surface ore, he felt sure of success.

But how could he interest capital? He had failed in other projects, and the world did not believe in him. In vain he besought men to join him. He hoarded his money, grew thin from lack of food, dressed in ragged clothes, and still dreamed of future success.

Finally a little money was put into the venture, but no veins worth working were found. Asa was sure they would win if they probed further into the mountain. He labored with men in and out of camp to put in more money. The miners said he was crazy. He certainly was cold and hungry, and well nigh frenzied.

At last he found a German, Hans Bochert, who, like himself, had struggled for years, had lost and won,—with many losings to one winning,—but who, out of pity for the old miner, gave nearly his last dollar to push on the work.

Asa seemed in a half delirium. He would not leave the place day or night. Cold or rain did not deter him, though he seemed ill and broken. Finally the good news came that a big body of ore was struck. Asa Scranton's face gleamed as though the full sunlight poured upon it. "I'm going to my shanty to write to Martha," he said, and hurried away. He did not come back in the morning, and Hans Bochert and the other men hastened over to know the reason.

Asa sat in his chair with the same halo about his face—dead from an excess of joy. On a paper, on the little table, was the letter he had begun to write to Martha Scranton at Fairport: "Darling Wife: I have struck it rich, and you and the children"—

The pen had fallen from his hand.

107

FOOD AT THE DOOR

"DON'T FEED him, because others will be sure to come."

The speaker was a handsome woman who sat at dinner with her husband in one of the beautiful homes of C. She was dressed in a rich garnet satin, with a bunch of yellow chrysanthemums at her throat, which accorded with the dark garnet leather of the carved furniture.

All had gone well with Mrs. Heatherstone. Her husband, with hair prematurely gray from his hard financial struggles, had become rich, and his wife and only son were spending the money in fine clothes and stylish equipages.

A servant had just come in to say that an old man was at the door who had had nothing to eat all day, and to ask if she should give him a supper.

Mrs. Heatherstone reiterated her old rule, not to feed anybody at the door, lest other poor people be told of it, and the family be annoyed with tramps. "We never give anything at the door," she was wont to say, and so in process of time poor people generally passed by the Heatherstone mansion, and she was glad of it.

The poor old man of to-night caught a glimpse of the well-filled table as he passed the window, and he felt hurt and bitter at fate. He was not a drinking man, but he had lost his property by reverses, his wife and children were dead, he was unable to do hard labor, and he could rarely find work that was light or heavy. There was not work enough for all, and the young and vigorous obtained what there was.

The old man slept in a shed that night, and dreamed of the elegant home and the handsome lady in the garnet dress.

"I think you might have given him a supper," said Mark Heatherstone, a boy of sixteen, with a kind heart, but lacking a strong will, and who had already caused his parents some solicitude.

"When once you begin, there is no end of it," said the mother. "Let him go to the Associated Charities or to some soup-house."

"But he will have a heavy heart to-night, besides being hungry," said the youth.

"I can't take care of all the suffering in the world, so I shut my eyes to it. We must enjoy ourselves, and leave some money for you also."

"I don't mind much about that," said the boy, who knew

108

nothing of the hardships of life, "but I'd do a little good as I went along."

Mother and son did not think alike about many things, and after a time the lad left his home and disappeared from the town.

His parents were of course distressed beyond measure. They searched and searched in vain. Mrs. Heatherstone, with all her selfishness and lack of wisdom in rearing her son, was exceedingly fond of him. His absence aged her, and when after some years he did not return, the fine house and elegant clothes lost their attraction. The habit of giving, however, is usually a growth from early life, and closed hands do not unclose easily as we grow older.

Once away from his home, Mark Heatherstone was too proud to go back, if indeed he ever wished to do so. He soon spent what money he had brought away with him, and then learned the hard lessons of poverty. He looked for work, occasionally found some, but oftener was penniless, and, like the old man who had besought alms at his father's house, slept in sheds or in barns. The increasing habit of drink fastened upon him, and exposure undermined his health.

Early a broken-down man, he determined to go back to his native town, and perhaps seek again the home he had abandoned. He stole a ride on a freight train and reached the city just as the evening lamps were being lighted. A cold sleet was falling.

He was faint from lack of food, and excited with the thought of the old times of boyhood and a possible glad reception at his home. He found the house, passed it, and saw his father and mother at supper. He went up the street and then returned, going to the back door and asking for food.

"We never give anything at the door," said the well-instructed servant, and shut it in his face. He walked away. The impulse was strong to go back and say that the long-lost son had returned. He hesitated, turned his face back towards home, walked up the familiar pathway to the front door, raised his hand to ring the bell, became dizzy, and fell heavily on the porch.

Mr. and Mrs. Heatherstone were startled at the sound. "What has happened, husband?" she said, and both hastened to the door. "Oh, Mark, Mark!" exclaimed the mother, as she gazed upon the face of her apparently dead son. He was carried into the best apartment and a physician summoned.

"It is a heart attack and he will rally," said the doctor, "but his living is only a question of time."

When Mark was partially restored to his former self he told of

109

the struggles he had been through, of some kindness and much indifference and hardness, even being turned away in the rain from his mother's door because he asked for food. "That nearly broke my heart, mother," he said. "Don't let man or dog or cat go away from your door hungry. Who knows but they will die upon somebody's doorstep?"

Mrs. Heatherstone grew tenderer with the coming months, and when Mark passed away she was a changed woman. She had been made unselfish through a great sorrow.

HOW THE DOG TAX WAS PAID

TWO LITTLE children, Annie and James, were picking up stray pieces of coal near the railroad, to carry to a very poor home. Suddenly they espied a black lump that looked like coal, only it moved. With childish curiosity they crept towards it and found a thin, frightened, hungry dog that had been crippled and beaten by boys.

"Do you dare touch her?" said the girl of nine years. "She might bite."

"Oh, yes," said Jimmie, a rugged and alert little fellow of seven. "See, she wags her short tail, and I guess she wants to go home with us."

"But mother couldn't take care of her, we're so poor, and baby Ned and Willie have to eat and have clothes."

"Oh, I'll give her some of my bread and milk every night, and Mrs. Martin next door will give her bones, I guess. She hasn't any boy and she is good to me."

The girl put her fingers carefully along the black dog's forehead, and the animal pushed her cold nose against the child's hand and licked it. She was not used to kind voices, and a girl's fingers upon her head gave her courage. She half rose to her feet, looked from one to the other and seemed to say, "I will go with you if you will only take me."

"I wouldn't pick her up, Jimmie; she'll follow us."

"She can't walk much," said the boy, "but I'll help her over the bad places if you'll carry the basket of coal."

The dog seemed to realize the conversation, for when the coal was ready to be moved, she was also ready, and hobbled on after the children.

"You must be tired, poor thing!" said Jimmie, taking her up as they crossed a muddy street, and thereby getting his torn jacket stained from her hurt back and bleeding foot.

The dog nestled up to him and seemed happy. When they reached home Jimmie ran ahead, showing his poor bruised friend to his mother.

"Why, Jimmie, what can you do with a dog?"

"Keep her to play with, and to guard the house when you are away washing."

"I don't know how we'll feed her," said Mrs. Conlon, who

111

looked about as poor as the dog, "but we'll try. We can keep her warm anyway if you'll pick up enough coal."

"We shall love her so," said the boy, "and the baby will play with her when she gets well. Let's call her 'Pet,' because we never have anything to play with."

The dog crawled behind the stove and closed her eyes, as though thankful for a place to rest, where at least boys would not throw stones, and men would not kick her with their rough boots.

Days and weeks went by. The black dog, though not having a great supply of food, was living like a prince compared with the starvation of the street. Her bruises healed, her coat became blacker and her eyes brighter. She was indeed the baby's pet, and the idol of the other children. She went with Annie and Jimmie as they gathered coal. She slept on the floor beside their humble bed at night, and guarded the household when the mother was absent. She shared their food, and would have returned their kindness with her life if need be. The whole family were happier and kinder since she came into it, as is always the case when a pet animal is in the home.

Though poverty was a constant guest at the Conlon abode, with its bare floors, poor clothes, and common fare, yet they were not unhappy. The mother worked too hard to philosophize much about circumstances, and the children were too young to realize what was before them of struggle. A cloud was coming, and a man's hand brought it. It was the arrival of the tax-gatherer.

A high official in the State found that the treasury was low, and decided that money must be raised in some way. Of course it was generally conceded that the liquor traffic caused so much of the poverty, crime, and sorrow that it would be wise to make it pay for some of its evil results. This was a difficult matter, however, as saloon keepers and their customers had votes. Corporations could be taxed more heavily, but corporations sometimes paid money to help carry elections.

There was at least one class that had no votes, and consequently little influence. Dogs could therefore be taxed. The rich could easily pay the tax, and if the poor could not, their dogs could be killed. Who stopped to think whether money raised through the sorrow of the poor, or the death of helpless animals, might prove a bane rather than a blessing? Who asked whether a dog did not love life as well as his master, and whether, for his devotion and courage and guarding of homes, he was not entitled to the consideration of the city and the State, rather than to be killed because his owner could not or did not pay a tax or a license fee?

112

The dog had done no wrong, and though somebody loved him, as he could not earn the fee himself he must needs be destroyed.

The tax-gatherer, endowed with power by the officials, came to the Conlon home. There was little that could be taken from so poor a place, thought the collector, until he espied the black dog beside the baby's cradle. "Your dog, madam, must be paid for. The fee is five dollars."

"I haven't the money," said the woman. "Why, I couldn't raise so much! I can hardly fill these four mouths with food."

"Well, madam, then you shouldn't keep a dog."

"But she guards the children while I work, and she is such a comfort to them!"

"The law doesn't take sentiment into the account. If you were a man I should arrest you, and shoot the dog. As it is, I will only shoot the dog. Bring the animal out and I will call that policeman over."

"You wouldn't shoot her before these crying children?"—for three of them had begun to cry, and were clasping the dog to their hearts, while the baby looked scared, and pressed his lips together, as though he realized that something was wrong.

"As I said before, madam, the law has no regard for sentiment. The State must have money."

"I wish they would tax the saloons. If my husband hadn't lost his money in them before he died we should have the money now to pay the tax for our dog. Could you wait a little for the money? I can give you a dollar, and perhaps I can borrow another, but I can't possibly raise five dollars. Can you come to-morrow?"

"Yes, I'll give you a trial, but it's a long walk here. I'm afraid you'll turn the dog on the street and then say you haven't any."

"Oh, no, sir, we are not as mean as that, even if we are poor! Pet would suffer and perhaps starve, and we all love her too much for that."

After the man was gone Mrs. Conlon put on her faded shawl and bonnet and went to her neighbors, as poor as herself. One loaned her a quarter, another a half, till the whole dollar was secured.

When the assessor came on the following day, being somewhat impressed by the devotion of both family and dog, he took the two dollars and promised to wait a reasonable time for the remaining three.

Various plans were talked over in the Conlon home for the raising of the extra money. There was comparatively little work to be obtained, rent must be met or they would be turned upon the street, and there were five mouths to feed besides that of Pet.

Jimmie declared that a letter to the Governor of the State ought to do good, and Annie should write it. Accordingly a sheet of paper and an envelope were procured that very afternoon, and a letter was penned to that official. It read as follows:

"Dear Mr. Governor:

"We have a beautiful this was a stretch of the imagination black dog that we found sick and hurt, and we love her dearly, but can't pay the tax of five dollars. Mother works, and I take care of the children, but I can't earn any money for poor dear Pet. The police have killed lots of dogs on our street. One belonged to Mamie Fisher, my best friend, and we went together and found him in a pile of dogs, all dead. Mamie took him up in her arms and cried dreadfully. I helped her carry him, and we dug a grave in their little yard and buried him, and we took five cents that a lady gave me and bought two roses and laid on his grave. He was a big yellow puppy, and was so kind.

"Now, Mr. Governor, would you be willing to lend us three dollars till we can earn it, and pay you back? She has two dollars already. We wish there wasn't any tax on dogs, for they make us poor children so happy. Perhaps you can stop the law.

"Yours most respectful,
"Annie Conlon."

All pronounced this a proper letter, and Jimmie dropped it into the mail-box. All the family waited prayerfully for the answer.

The Governor was touched as he read this letter from a child. "I will give her the three dollars," he said to his wife. "I didn't suppose the enforcement of a dog tax would bring so much sorrow to little hearts and large ones too. I really wish there were no tax on dogs, for they are helpless creatures and most faithful friends to man. But the State needs money."

"Try to get the tax law repealed," said the wife. "There are plenty of ways to raise money to pay the expenses of a great State without killing dogs. The tax law is directly responsible for thousands of dogs being turned upon the street to starve: they become ill from hunger and thirst, are supposed to be mad, and then suffer untold misery and even death from thoughtless and excited crowds. I would have no part in enforcing such a law, and would help to wipe it from the statute books."

114

"But some of the farmers have their sheep killed by dogs, and they must have their losses made up to them," said the Governor.

"Let the town pay for the sheep which are killed, and not cause the death of thousands of innocent dogs because a few have done wrong," replied the wife.

The money was sent to Annie Conlon, and there was thanksgiving in the plain home. Pet wagged her short tail, and looked up into Annie's eyes, as though she understood that her life had been spared by those three dollars.

THE STORY OF DOUGLAS

DOUGLAS was a shaggy black puppy, one of a family of eleven, all of them yellow and white but himself. His fur, when you pushed it apart, showed its yellow color near the skin, revealing what he really was,—a St. Bernard.

He was the most gentle of all the puppies, and would not fight his way at the dish when the others clamored for their bread and milk, but stood apart and looked up to his mistress with a beseeching and sometimes aggrieved air. From the first he seemed to hunger for human affection, and would cry to be held in one's lap, or follow one about the house or the grounds like a petted kitten.

When quarrels took place between some members of the large family Douglas never joined, but hastened to tell it by his bark, that the disturbance might be quelled. When finally the puppies went to various homes Douglas became the property of a lady who, not having children, loved him almost as a child.

He followed her up and down stairs and lay at her feet if she read. The house was well furnished, but not too good to be used and enjoyed. Douglas was not put out of doors at night to whine in the rain or sleet, or even into a barn, and wisely, for he saved the house once from very unwelcome intruders.

He gambolled beside his mistress if she walked in the woods, and when she was ill he was constantly at her bedside, refusing to eat, and seeming to suffer in her suffering. When she was unavoidably absent Douglas cried and walked the floor, and if allowed to go out of doors howled and waited on the hillside for her return.

Once when at the seashore he followed her without her knowledge, and plunged into the bay after her steamer. He swam till well-nigh exhausted, his agonized owner fearing every minute that he would sink, while she besought the men to stop the boat. Finally he was rescued, and though he could scarcely move the glad look in his eyes and the wag of his tail told as plainly as words the joy of the reunion.

No amount of money could buy the companionable creature. He never wearied one by talk; he never showed anger, perhaps because no one spoke angrily to him. Some persons like to show authority, even over a dog, and talk loud and harsh, but Douglas's owner was too wise and too good for this. Kindness begot kindness, and the puppy who longed for love appreciated it none the less when he was grown, and could protect the woman who loved him.

One autumn day, just before leaving her country home for the city, Miss Benson was obliged to return to town for a half day. "Good-by, dear Douglas," she said in her usual way. "I shall come home soon," and the unwilling creature followed her with his brown eyes, and whined that he could not go also. Later in the afternoon he was let out of doors, and soon disappeared.

When Miss Benson returned her first word was, "Douglas! Douglas!" but there was no response to her call. He had followed her, had lost the trail, and had gone too far to find his way back to his home. In vain she called for her pet. She left the door ajar, hoping at nightfall she should hear the patter of his feet, or his eager bark to come in, but he did not come. She wondered where he slept, if he slept at all; thought a dozen times in the night that she heard him crying at the door; imagined him moaning for her, or, supperless and exhausted, lying down by the roadside, to wait for the sunrise to begin his fruitless journey.

Douglas had become that sad thing, a lost dog. He belonged to nobody now, and both owner and dog were desolate. Miss Benson could scarcely go about her work. She spent days in searching, and hired others to search, but all was useless. For weeks she thought Douglas might possibly come back. If she could know that he was dead, that even would be a consolation; but to fear he was cold and hungry, to realize that the world is all too indifferent to animals, unless perchance they are our own, to imagine he might be in some medical college, the victim of the surgeon's knife,—all this was bitter in the extreme. Weeping and searching did no good, and finally the inevitable had to be accepted, though the sadness in Miss Benson's heart did not fade out.

As is ever the case, those of us who have lost something precious become more tender and helpful in a world full of losses. Miss Benson welcomed and cared for every stray animal that she found, perhaps never quite giving up the hope that she would see gentle, great-hearted Douglas again.

And what of Douglas? He ran fast at first, eager to overtake the one to whom he was passionately devoted. She had been gone so long that he soon lost track of her footsteps, and then with a dazed look he began to howl, hoping that she would hear his voice. He lay down to rest, but it was growing dark and he was hungry.

He stopped at a large house and the servants drove him away. He was unused to this, but he dragged himself along to the next place. Here a kind woman gave him something to eat, and would have made him welcome for the night, but he would not stay after he had eaten. He must needs wander on, hoping to find his home and his beloved mistress. All night long he tramped, lying down now and then by the side of the road to rest a few minutes.

The next day was a hard one. He was beginning to realize that he was lost. He ran more slowly, looked eagerly at every passer-by, and seemed half demented. At night he stopped at a home where the lights had just been lighted, and some pretty children seemed flitting from room to room. He whined at the back door.

A flaxen-haired little girl opened it. "Oh, mamma," said the child, "here is a big black dog, and I know he is hungry! May I feed him?"

"No," replied the woman, "take a whip and send him off. I will have no lean stray dogs about this house."

"But he looks hungry, mother," pleaded little Emma Bascomb, "and I know he won't bite."

Mrs. Bascomb, pity it is to tell it, was a very pious person, never failing to be present at prayer-meetings, always deeply interested in the heathen, and most helpful at sewing societies of the church. She never fed stray cats or dogs, as she did not wish them to stay at her house. She did not remember that God made them, and that He lets not a sparrow fall to the ground without His notice, and she forgot that she was to emulate Him.

Mrs. Bascomb varied her treatment of stray dogs and cats. Sometimes she used a long black whip, sometimes pails of water. On this occasion she threw on Douglas, already weak and hungry, a pail of cold water, and sent him frightened and hurt away from her door. Emma protested. "When I have a home of my own, mamma," she said, "I will never turn away a dog or a cat hungry." The child knew that it was useless to say more, as a stray cat had stayed about the house for a week, and Mrs. Bascomb had refused to feed it, burning up the scraps from the table lest some starving animal might be tempted to remain. And yet the Bascombs had family prayers, and asked God to provide clothes for the needy and food for the hungry!

Douglas was beginning to learn the sorrows of the poor and homeless. He longed to see some familiar face, to hear some familiar voice. He went on and on, and it began to rain. It was almost sleet, and the dog, used to a warm fire, shivered and longed for shelter. Approaching a large rambling house with a shed attached, Douglas ran under it for cover, and crouched down at the side under a bench. A man came out with a lamp. Evidently he had

118

been drinking, for his step was unsteady. He had come out to close the shed door, and espying the dog gave him a kick with his hard boot.

"Get out, you scoundrel! What are you doing here?" he said gruffly, and poor Douglas ran as though a gun had been fired at him.

"Oh, if there were only a home for such lost ones!" he must have thought; but there was none, and again the hungry and wet dog travelled on. A wagon soon passed with two men in it, and Douglas followed, hoping it would lead to a home for him. "Whip him off," said one of the men to the other. "We've got two dogs already, and my wife would never allow a third," and they brandished the whip in the rear and drove on. Douglas crawled under a tree, and rolling himself as nearly as he could into a round ball for warmth finally fell asleep.

In the morning he started again on his toilsome journey. He was lame now and half sick. Soon the houses were nearer together, and Douglas realized that he was coming into a city. He did not know there was little room for dogs in an overcrowded, fashionable city. There was little green grass to roam over, and the rushing world did not want the bother of animals. Perhaps, however, where there were so many people there would be some kind hearts, he thought.

He crept along and looked into the window of a restaurant. There was a boiled ham in the window, cake, pies, and other attractive things. He wagged his tail a little, and looked into a man's face as he went in, but the man paid no attention. Then a young lady passed, and she said, "Poor dog!" but went on.

Douglas walked away and lay down in front of a store, but a man came and said, "Get out! The ladies will be afraid of you."

Douglas looked no longer the petted, handsome creature of several days before. The dust had settled in his black hair, which looked rough and coarse. He was thin and dejected. An unthinking boy chased him, and threw something at him, and as he was too peaceable to resent it he hurried along an alley and tried to hide up a stairway. A big red-faced man came out of a room at the head of the stairs and kicked him down the steps.

Douglas ran into a shoe-store. Three men cornered him with a broom and a pole, and one man, braver than the others, put a cloth over his head, and then seized him by the hind legs and threw him into the street. Then somebody on the sidewalk said, "That dog acts strangely. He must be mad!"

That was enough to excite the passers-by, who had read in the papers various accounts of supposed cases of rabies. "He is weak," said one person, "and he totters." "He is frothing at the mouth," said another. A boot-black ran after him and threw his box at the thoroughly frightened animal. A crowd gathered, and ran and shouted. "Shoot him! Shoot him!" was the eager cry.

Douglas did indeed froth at the mouth from excessive running. A lady hurried along and said, "Let me have the dog. He is not mad, but has lost his owner. Frothing at the mouth is not a sign of hydrophobia, as the best physicians will tell you."

"No, madam," said a looker-on. "Don't touch the dog. We men will not allow you to be bitten."

A policeman fired his pistol, and the ball entered Douglas's shoulder. Half dead with pain as well as fright, the dog rushed on and finally escaped.

He lay in his hiding-place till midnight, and then when no human eye could see him he crept away from the city. If only Miss Benson could see him now, and dress his wounds, and say the petting words of old that he had so loved to hear!

Towards morning, exhausted, he lay down by the fence in the front yard of a house in the outskirts of the city. The owner of the home was a lawyer, a kind-hearted man, in part because he had a noble mother and wife.

"There's a poor wounded dog on our lawn, Jeannette," Mr. Goodman said to his wife. "Call him in at the back door, and we'll see if we can't help him."

Mrs. Goodman took a basin of warm water and castile soap and carefully washed the wound, the children standing about and anxiously watching the operation. "Nice dog," said Teddy, a boy of five. "He no bite."

"No," said his mother, as Douglas looked pitifully up into her face. "He is a kind dog, and must belong to a good home somewhere."

After she had finished washing the sore and tender place Douglas licked her hand in appreciation. "Have Dr. Thayer come in,"—he was the veterinary surgeon,—said Mrs. Goodman to her husband. "We might as well make the care of animals a part of our missionary work in the world. The doctor will find the ball, if it is still there, and save the dog, I hope."

"All right, wife," said Mr. Goodman, as he started for the office.

"I suppose you want some breakfast, doggie," said Mrs.

120

Goodman, and she placed before Douglas a dish of meat and of milk. Douglas was too tired and too full of pain to eat much, but he felt as though a new world had opened to him. After all, there were some good people in the land, and at last he had reached them.

Dr. Thayer came, found the ball in the patient, abused animal, and the wounded shoulder soon began to heal.

When night came Mrs. Goodman made Douglas a warm bed of blankets by the kitchen stove, for she knew that a cold kennel was not a suitable place for him. Later he was washed and dried, by rubbing with cloths, till his coat was silky and black.

Teddy and the dog became inseparable companions. Wherever the child went Douglas was always close behind him, now licking his extended hand, now lying down for the child to clamber over him, or to lay his dark curls against the darker curls of the dog. They shared their food, and they frequently went to sleep together, if it could be called sleep on the part of the dog, whose eyes were usually open that his little charge might be guarded. Douglas never showed an inclination to bite unless some one touched the boy, and then he growled and looked concerned.

One summer day Teddy and a playmate wandered off with the dog during Mrs. Goodman's absence. They sat down under a tree and all three lunched together. Then they played along the meadow till the banks of a river were reached. Two men were working near by and occasionally watched the children at their play, as they dabbled their hands in the water. Finally they heard a child scream, and before they could reach the place Douglas was dragging Teddy, dripping and frightened, from the river. The men carried the boy home to his awe-struck but overjoyed parents, and Douglas, wet and excited, was praised for his heroic conduct.

A year later, when Teddy went to school, Douglas missed his comrade, and for days whined piteously. He never failed to go, at the regular hour for closing school, to meet his little friend, and always brought home in his teeth the dinner basket of the lad. Sometimes Douglas whined in his sleep, as though he were dreaming of other days, but love for Teddy made him, on the whole, very happy.

When Teddy was seven years old diphtheria raged in the school, and marked him for one of its victims. No love or care could save him.

When conscious, he could not bear Douglas out of his sight or reach. As in the case with his former mistress, Douglas neither ate nor slept. When all was over he disappeared. Where he went nobody knew. Probably he lay upon the grave of the child, and later wandered off, thinking perchance to find again his first love.

The Goodmans had intended to leave their home in the suburbs and move to the city before their boy died, and now Mrs. Goodman was anxious to go away from the place as quickly as possible. A home was soon obtained, and the family moved thither. They deeply regretted that Douglas could not be found to go with them, because they were much attached to him for his own sake, and because he was so dear to their child.

Douglas meantime had hunted far and wide for his lost ones. He had the same bitter experience of neglect and hunger, but a dog's love is his strongest quality, and despite suffering he was seeking his own. Miss Benson he could not find; that was past hope, but Teddy, perhaps, he might see again. Probably Douglas did not know that death has no awakening in this world, and that Teddy could never come to his home, but the dog finally stole back to the porch and yard where they had played together and waited, hoping that the boy would come. The house was vacant. Some neighbors saw him on the steps, but he went away again. Finally a policeman saw him and heard him howl.

"Whose dog is that?" he said to a neighbor.

"It's a dog that came to the Goodmans and disappeared when their little boy died. I suppose he has come back to find the child," was the reply.

"Ah!" said the man, "and he hasn't any collar on his neck. He is unlicensed. I will send the Society for the Prevention of Cruelty to Animals after him."

"I'll see that he doesn't starve," said the woman. "Will the Society find a home for him?"

"Oh, no, they can't find homes for so many as they take off the streets! They'll kill him."

"He isn't to blame for not being licensed. I don't see the use of the license law, because it means the death of so many thousands of animals."

"Neither do I," said the kind-hearted policeman. "Poor folks can't always pay the fee. I love my dog, and he's a great comfort to my children. But I don't make the law. I only help to enforce it."

"What is done with the license money? It makes so much heartache it ought to do great good."

"I've heard that it is given sometimes to public schools and to libraries to buy books on kindness to animals, and sometimes to the Humane Society so that they can pay men to catch and kill unlicensed dogs. You see, the licensed dogs help to kill the unlicensed and homeless," said the man.

"I should think a better way would be to provide homes for the really homeless instead of killing them. I think that we have a duty to animals, seeing that they are under our protection."

The policeman told the S. P. C. A. that a black unlicensed dog was howling on the steps of a vacant house because his little friend had died. Two officers in a big wagon hastened to the spot, caught him, and threw him in with a score of other animals which they had seized on the street.

Douglas cowered in the corner, and wondered what new sorrow had befallen him. The other poor things were as frightened as himself. Two were black and white puppies scarcely bigger than kittens, and two were pretty black-and-tan pets. A large mastiff looked out of her great brown eyes, trembling from head to foot. One shepherd dog was poor and thin, but most looked well cared for, only they had no collars, and their owners had not paid their license fee.

The wagon soon reached a barn-like structure, and the animals were hastily emptied into a pen with sawdust on the floor. What was in store for them they could only guess. After a time they were offered a mixture of meal and meat, but most were too frightened to eat.

All the next day they listened for footsteps, hoping that some friend would come for them. Douglas lay in the corner and expected nobody. Miss Benson did not know where he was, and Teddy had never come back when he howled for him.

There was a large pen adjoining that of Douglas, and this was filled with dogs—fox-terriers, some black like himself, and several yellow ones. Cats, many of them large and handsome, were in cages about the room. Some animals had been brought to the pound, or refuge, by persons who did not or could not take the trouble to find homes for them. An advertisement in the paper saying that a dog had been found and would be given to a good home would in almost every case have met with responses, but this cost a little money and time.

A boy brought in two pretty creatures, one red and the other yellow, which he said he had found without collars. A woman had hired him and other children by paying each a few cents to do this work, which meant almost certain death to animals, believing, probably, that she was doing good.

Late in the afternoon Douglas witnessed a strange, sad sight.

123

Every cat, fifty or more, was thrown into a large cage, and poisonous gas turned in upon them. The terrified creatures huddled together, as though they knew their helplessness in the hands of their destroyers, and died.

Then several men, as soon as the cats were removed, threw the shrinking, crying dogs into the cage, and they too were soon dead, piled upon each other. Douglas and the rest knew that their turn would come soon.

On the second day a lady called at the refuge because her own city contemplated establishing a home (?) where dogs could be killed, the license fees to be used to pay the salaries of the S. P. C. A. agents. Her heart was touched by the appealing looks of the helpless animals. She went away and found homes for two fox-terriers, paid the license fees and fines, and the dogs were released, licking her hands, as though they realized from what they had been saved.

Douglas crept towards the visitor, because he had been used to a woman's voice. He was thin, but his eyes were as beautiful as when he was a puppy and responded to the petting of Miss Benson's gentle hands.

"You have been a handsome dog," the lady said to Douglas, "and somebody has loved you. I know of a place for you. A noble woman who loves dogs has provided a home for the homeless, as far as her means will allow, and is devoting her life to the care of such of God's creatures as you are. Would you like to go with me?"

Douglas whined, and the other poor animals crowded around as much as to say, "Can you not take us too, and save us from death to-morrow? We cannot pay the license, but we would love and protect anybody who would pay it and take us home." The lady could not take them all—the city and State, by reason of their wealth and humaneness, instead of license or tax, should provide homes for those committed to their keeping by the Creator. Douglas was let out, and followed the lady with a thankful heart, but with a downcast look, as though life had been so uncertain that he could not be sure of anything good in the future.

The lady hired a cab, and the dog lay at her feet. They were driven to an attractive-looking brick house, with several small buildings adjoining. A young girl came to the door.

"Do you wish to see the matron of the Dogs' Home?" said the girl.

"Yes, I am a friend of the matron," said the lady, "and I have taken a fancy to a homeless dog and have brought him here to find a home."

The matron soon appeared, and, with one wild cry, Douglas

124

sprang into her arms. It was Miss Benson, who, since she had lost Douglas, had been moved to spend her life and her fortune for other dogs who were lost.

"Oh, Douglas! Douglas!" she exclaimed, while the visitor looked on with amazement. "Have you found me and I you at last?" And the dog whined and caressed her till she feared he would die from excess of joy unless she calmed him.

"You and I will never be parted again. You shall live here and help care for other lost and unwanted ones."

For years Douglas thankfully shared in the care and love of his mistress. She could not bear to see him grow old, but he had suffered too much to live to the usual age of St. Bernards. When he died his head was in Miss Benson's lap, and his great brown eyes looked upon her face and whitening hair as the last precious thing to be seen in life. She buried him and laid flowers upon his grave, for was he not her devoted, loyal friend? A neat headstone tells where faithful Douglas sleeps.